LUKE
ON
ALCATRAZ

ARTHUR FLYNN

MENTOR
BOOKS

This Edition first published 2002 by

MENTOR BOOKS
43 Furze Road,
Sandyford Industrial Estate,
Dublin 18.

Tel. (01) 295 2112/3   Fax. (01) 295 2114
e-mail: all@mentorbooks.ie

ISBN: 1-84210-021-1

A catalogue record for this book is available from the
British Library

Cover Illustration: Jon Berkeley
Typesetting, editing, design and layout by Mentor Books
Printed in Ireland by ColourBooks

1 3 5 7 9 10 8 6 4 2

Contents

The Author

Arthur Flynn

Arthur Flynn lives in Bray, County Wicklow. He is the Honorary Secretary of the Irish centre of International PEN and is the Treasurer of the Society of Irish Playwrights.

He has written a number of radio plays including *To Scare a Spook*, *Remember Me* and *Mysterious Mr Maxwell*. He also has written many children's plays for radio including the Captain Mungo series. For television he has written scripts for *Bosco*, *Wanderly Wagon*, *Fortycoats* and *The Live Mike*.

He is the author of several books including *Echoes* (1978), *Irish Dance* (1981), *History of Bray* (1986), *Irish Film: 100 Years* (1996), and his first books with Mentor, *Achill Adventure* (1997), *Luke's Heroes* (1998) and *Luke in the Movies* (1999).

Dedicated to

Ben,
who will provide a lot more inspiration

1

THE INVITATION

'I could have guessed it was you,' said Mrs Carroll, coming in from the back garden, with a basket of washing. 'You hit the place like a hurricane.'

'I'm in a hurry,' mumbled Luke through a mouthful of apple and yoghurt. 'I've got to get a move on.'

'What's new . . . you're always in a panic,' smiled his mother. 'Where's that scruffy football gear of yours?'

'Don't know . . . suppose it's in my kit bag,' he replied, not too concerned.

She nodded. 'Oh, go on. I'll find it. I'd hate to ruin your social life.' Luke licked the edge of the yoghurt carton as he headed for the door. 'Oh Luke, just one other thing,' she called as he vanished out the door.

He stuck his freckled face around the door and moaned impatiently, 'Ah, what now, Mam? Will you get off my case. I'm late.'

'There's a letter for you,' she said, nodding towards the letter rack on top of the fridge.

Luke cautiously approached the fridge, fearing that it might be a note from the school. Now that he was back in school after the long summer holidays, it might be the first of many notes sent home by his teachers. They could instantly supply a list of complaints about his behaviour and performance.

'Who's it from?' he asked, barely audible.

'You'll have to open it to find out, but there's an American stamp on it,' said his mother, also curious to discover its contents.

Luke took down the letter. His red head bowed, he scanned the typed name and address and inspected the American stamp before turning over the envelope.

His mother was amused. 'You'll have to *open* it to find out.'

'Oh yeah,' he answered. Slowly he began to tear open the envelope. He removed a single typed sheet and began to read it.

'Well?' said his mother with her hands on her hips. 'Don't keep me in suspense.'

Luke's face and actions became more animated as he read down the page, 'Just . . . just a sec . . . it's from Todd . . . he wants us . . . yes, yes . . . yippee . . .' he roared, flinging the letter into the air.

With a puzzled expression his mother stooped to pick the sheet of paper up. 'You're not making any sense, Luke.'

'Can I go? Can I go?' pleaded Luke tugging at his mother's sleeve.

'If you let me read the letter I might be able to give you an answer,' she replied, holding the page between her two hands. Her lips moved as she read it to herself. Luke impatiently hopped from one foot to the other waiting for her to finish.

There was an expression of astonishment on his mother's face as she lowered the letter onto the table. 'It's from your friend Todd . . . he's so generous and thoughtful. He's invited us all out to San Francisco for the premiere of the film they made here last year.'

By now Luke's face was beaming with the news. 'I know all that, Mam, but can I go?'

Memories of the fun he and his two pals, Sticky and Damian, had experienced the previous summer working as extras for Ardmore Studios came flooding back. But making friends with the leading child star, Todd Harper, had been the best part of all. The film, *Orphans' Retreat* was opening in the States and now Todd had invited them all out to the premiere.

'But there's so much we'll have to discuss first . . . with your dad . . . and the school . . . and the other lads' parents . . . we've got . . .' said his mother as she tried to absorb the news.

'What are you like, Mam? You never let me go anywhere. Everybody else has been to Spain and America and everywhere but I never go anywhere. It's not fair,' said Luke beginning to sulk.

'That's not true, Luke. We go on holidays every year,' said his mother sympathetically.

'Yeah, to poxy old Kerry and Galway. That's not a proper holiday . . . but San Francisco . . . that's deadly . . . massive . . . car chases and earthquakes and everything.'

There was no pleasing him now. He only wanted to hear one thing. His mother couldn't resist smiling.

'Luke, I didn't say you couldn't go. I'd love for you to go and me as well. Sure my cousin Deirdre is out there and I haven't seen her in over ten years. It would be a great treat.'

Luke scratched his head. 'I don't get you. One minute you're saying I can't go. Now you're saying maybe I can. Which is it?'

'Ah Luke, you're getting on my nerves now. We've only

9

just got the letter. Tell you what . . . I'll discuss it with your dad and we'll see what we can work out,' she said quietly, trying not to dampen his enthusiasm.

Luke's eyes narrowed as he picked up the letter again.

'I still don't get you. Can I show this to the lads?'

'Sure, it's your letter,' she nodded.

Excitedly Luke read the letter again and examined the envelope and date stamp. 'I honestly thought he'd forget about us once he was back with all those film stars and all.'

'Just goes to show how wrong you can be about people,' said his mother leaning thoughtfully against the draining board. 'And Luke, I'm sure we can work something out.'

'You really think so?' he replied, still reeling from the news. 'It would be—'

Before he had finished speaking the doorbell rang. He darted through the house to answer it. He swung the hall door open and waved the letter in the air as Damian and Sticky stood staring at him. His sister, Barbara, was coming up the path behind them.

'You'll never guess what's happened?' cried Luke.

Sticky made a face. 'Eh . . . your cat has died.'

'You got a new pair of boots,' guessed Damian.

'You're showing off again,' snapped Barbara.

The grin on Luke's face widened as he teased them. 'Not in a million years will you guess what it is.'

Sticky was growing impatient. 'Are you going to tell us or what?'

Luke took a deep breath and announced in a loud voice, 'Todd Harper has invited us all over to America for the premiere of *Orphans' Retreat*.'

'Will you come off it. You don't expect us to fall for that one,' said Damian shaking his head, his mop of fair hair

10

sticking out at all angles.

'You're a desperate spoofer, Carroll,' laughed Sticky. 'Try pulling the other one.'

Barbara brushed by them into the hall. 'Luke Carroll, you're the greatest liar that ever lived.'

'That shook you all, because it's true,' said Luke in a confident tone. 'I have the letter. Just listen.'

Dear Luke,

I hope you and all my friends in Bray – Damian, Sticky and of course, Barbara – are keeping well. Since I got back home I have been working on another film in LA called *The Brave Kid*. At least the clothes are modern. No bare feet or rags in this film. As you all treated me so well while I was in Bray I would like to invite you Luke, Barbara, your parents and yes, you too Sticky and Damian to San Francisco next month for the World Premiere of *Orphans' Retreat*. Don't worry about the cost. I will organise your tickets, accommodation, etc. I hope you can all make it. It should be great fun and I can show you what life is like out here.

My parents are so looking forward to meeting you. Really try hard to get over here. My mom says that she will ring your mom in a few days and they will sort out the details. I will call you too. All the best, gang. Hope to see you soon.

Todd.

'Wow, let me see that,' exclaimed Sticky, grabbing the letter. 'Is it for real?'

'Careful, don't tear it,' yelled Luke, as he passed the page over.

Sticky stared at the letter in disbelief. 'Does . . . does he

11

really mean he wants all of us to go?'

'Yeah, of course . . . we're all invited to San Francisco . . . isn't it deadly?' said Luke, in an excited voice.

As Sticky lowered the letter his face held a disappointed expression. 'But it's on the other side of the world. How are we going to get there?'

Barbara tapped him on the head. 'You eejit . . . did you never hear of a plane? You didn't expect to drive, did you?'

'But . . .' he began sounding despondent.

'A plane would be brill,' said Luke, still high with the excitement.

Sticky shook his head. 'Sounds deadly but I won't be able to go.'

Barbara seemed puzzled. 'But why can't you? We all want to.'

Sticky bit his lower lip before speaking. 'But my old man's not working. I couldn't afford to go. He wouldn't have the money'

Luke gave him a dig in the arm. 'Do you never listen to anything? It sounds like Todd's going to pay for everything – and I mean *everything*.'

Sticky screwed up his face. 'But that'll still cost a bomb . . . all the way to America . . . are you serious?'

Luke began to sound doubtful. 'Wait till I see what it says . . . eh . . . yeah, here it is . . . "I will organise tickets, accommodation, etc." There you have it. That's good enough for me.'

'Hang on a sec,' began Damian. 'He says he'll organise everything but he doesn't say he'll pay for it.'

Barbara rubbed her chin. 'That's right. It could mean he'll make the arrangements but we might have to pay ourselves.'

Luke stamped his foot impatiently. 'No way, Todd's not like that. I bet you anything he's going to pay the lot. He's filthy rich. Worth millions.'

'I hope you're right because I'd give anything to be able to go,' said Sticky, with a dreamy expression.

'There's nothing definite yet. We'll have to find out what the parents say,' said Luke, folding the letter and returning it to the envelope.

For the rest of the day Luke day-dreamed about San Francisco. As geography was his weakest subject he had to look up his atlas to discover where San Francisco was situated. It was on the west coast of North America.

At tea time in the Carroll house the letter from Todd was the main topic of conversation. The single sheet of paper was passed from one to the other and each of the foursome read and reread it.

'It would be a once in a lifetime opportunity,' said Luke's mother, choosing her words carefully. 'When we've checked out the details with Todd's parents and if it's genuine, I think we should try and let them go. We couldn't turn it down.'

'We wouldn't both be able to go,' said Mr Carroll as he poured the tea. 'The coffee shop has to be looked after. You go with them and I'll stay here.' The Carrolls owned and ran a coffee shop in Bray.

Luke grabbed his hand excitedly. 'You mean we're going then? I can't wait.'

His father waved his hand. 'Steady now, Luke. Nothing is definite until we speak to Todd's parents. Then we'll make a decision.'

'Can I tell my friends?' asked Barbara.

Her parents exchanged glances. 'Just wait until we've

confirmed it with the Harpers,' began her mother. 'It might only be Todd's idea.'

'That's true,' insisted Luke, through a mouthful of potato. 'But I'm sure Todd will come up with a plan. He's great at that.'

Luke and his pals didn't have long to wait to get confirmation of the invitation. The following night there was a phone call.

'Sounds like an American,' said Mr Carroll, as he called Luke to the phone.

Luke charged out to the hall. 'Bet you anything it's Todd.' His heart was pounding as he took the receiver from his father. 'Hello . . . oh Todd . . . yeah . . . it's deadly . . . I did, yeah . . . it's massive . . . I couldn't believe it . . . you really want us to go to San Francisco . . . yeah, yeah . . . sure . . . I can't wait . . . it's the best thing ever . . .'

Luke sat on the bottom step of the stairs to continue the conversation. Barbara and his parents gathered around. After talking for a few minutes Luke held the receiver away from himself. 'Todd's mam wants to talk to one of you.'

His parents looked from one to the other before his mother said, 'Give it to me.' She spoke into the phone. 'Hello, this is Luke's mother . . . oh, Mrs Harper . . . it's so nice to talk to you . . . yes, yes . . . we got the letter . . . it's so thoughtful . . . the children are over the moon . . . you're sure it's not any bother? . . . yes . . . and the expense? . . . yes, yes . . . I understand . . . that's wonderful to hear . . . well I think I'll be able to go . . . we both couldn't get away . . . I don't know how we can ever thank you enough . . . it's a treat of a lifetime. Indeed, I'll send you all the details. And thank you again. Good bye and God bless.'

She hung up looking pleased and content. Luke's eyes widened, 'Well?'

His mother smiled. 'Well Todd's offer is genuine. Mrs Harper confirmed the details. There won't be any costs involved except our own spending money. We'll be staying in their house and the film company will be covering the airfares and other expenses.'

'Fantastic!' shouted Luke. 'San Franscisco, here we come.'

Barbara smiled broadly. 'Then it's true. We can really go?'

Her mother nodded. 'Looks like it. I'll have to get myself something to wear . . . and buy some nice presents to bring out.'

'Before that we have to get together with the other lads' parents and see if they're agreeable,' said Mr Costello.

'True, let's draw up a list,' she agreed, picking up a pen and pad beside the phone.

The family of four sat around the kitchen table. Excitement rising, they began compiling a list of things that had to be done. Heading the list was 'organise passports' as only the parents had them. When they checked the calender to see what dates were involved, Mrs Carroll discovered a problem. 'OK, wait, what have we got here?' she said to herself.

Luke looked puzzled. 'What's up?'

'It means having to take eight days off school. That could be a problem,' she answered.

'Oh deadly,' began Luke, but quickly changed his tack. 'But I promise I'll work twice as hard in school if you let me go.'

His mother ruffled his red hair and laughed. 'Luke, this

is your mother you're talking to. Would you ever put that in writing.'

Luke blushed and they all laughed.

That night Sticky and Damian's parents were invited around to the Carroll's house to discuss the trip to San Francisco. By the end of the evening it was agreed that all four children could go.

2
THE TRIP

Over the next few weeks a lot of arrangements had to be made. Mr Carroll sorted out the passports. Luke, Barbara and the two boys began getting their savings together. One evening after tea the gang sat around the kitchen table. Luke's mother handed each of them an envelope.

'Now will you each tell me how much spending money you have?' asked Mrs Carroll as she held a biro over a sheet of paper.

'I've got €155,' boasted Luke.

Barbara looked smug and announced, '€184'.

'You would,' muttered Luke.

'Give over sniping, you pair,' snapped their mother. 'Damian, what have you got?'

'€130.'

'Good.'

They all waited for Sticky to speak. His cheeks reddened. Finally he announced softly, '€102'.

'That's fine. Now will you all write your initials on these envelopes and put the money into them,' instructed Mrs Carroll.

'How many dollars will we get?' enquired Luke.

His mother was thoughtful. 'I'd say it's about one to one at the moment. One euro gets you one dollar.'

'Deadly', exclaimed Barbara, 'That means I'll have $184.'

'Eh . . . yeah, something like that,' nodded her mother.

Luke rubbed his nose. 'Boy, that's stacks. We'll be able to buy lashings of gear. I can't wait.'

Barbara made a face at him. 'But I've got the most money. That shook you.'

'Barbara, enough of that,' said her mother crossly as she examined her notes. 'We want no bickering, do you hear me? Now listen. You're all going to need money belts, sunblock, sunglasses if you have them, headgear . . . oh, and something to read on the plane.'

'I don't get it, Mrs Carroll,' said Damian. 'If we have sunblock why do we need headgear? Surely it won't be sunny and wet at the same time?'

She laughed. 'A good question, Damian, but the sun is much warmer than here and you'll have to protect your head.'

Damian still seemed puzzled. 'Oh, I see.'

'Tell us, what's a money belt for, Mrs Carroll?' enquired Sticky.

'You eejit,' said Luke squeezing his friend's nose. 'Do you know nothing? You tie it around your waist and put your money in it.'

'But what's wrong with your pockets?' asked Sticky, with a confused expression. 'That's where I always keep my cash.'

Mrs Carroll tapped the table with her biro. 'Will you lot stop messing around. I'm trying to get things organised. You'll get me muddled. What next? Oh yes . . . just take one suitcase each and as few clothes as you can.'

'Do we take our togs?' asked Damian.

She scratched her chin with the pen. 'I'm not sure. I suppose so. They don't take up much space. And bring a

18

camera if you have one. If not you can always buy a disposable one. Anymore questions?'

'How far is San Francisco?' enquired Sticky.

Mrs Carroll wasn't sure, 'I didn't get time . . .'

'I know,' declared Barbara in her know-all voice, producing a sheet of paper. 'From Dublin to San Francisco is 2,830 kilometres, the population in 2000 was 776,773 and the average temperature is 73°F or 23°C. Anything else?'

Sticky and Damian exchanged glances. 'How do you know all that?' asked Sticky.

Mrs Carroll tapped Barbara on the head. 'Don't mind her. She got it all on the Internet.'

'Ah Mam, why did you have to go and spoil it?' moaned Barbara, folding the printout.

'How long does it take to get there?' asked Damian.

Mrs Carroll raised her eyebrows. 'That's the worst part of it. It's a long journey. We have to take two planes. The first one is to London and then from there we fly direct to San Francisco.'

Luke nibbled his bottom lip. 'But that's daft. I don't get it. You have to go in one direction and then the other. It's like going backwards and then forwards.'

'Sorry about that but there's no direct flight from Dublin,' smiled his mother.

'Will it be warm out there?' asked Sticky.

Mrs Carroll nodded. 'It should be hot enough for shorts and T-shirts.'

'Boy, that's far hotter than here,' cheered Luke. 'Even in summer. Can I go swimming?'

'We'll see,' replied his mother. 'Let's get out there first.'

They went on to discuss various other aspects of the

journey and live out fantasies of what they would see and experience in California. Mrs Carroll slipped away to continue with the packing.

Over the next few days all the arrangements were checked and double checked. Extra suitcases and bags were bought or borrowed. A few extra shorts and T-shirts were purchased for the children.

The best piece of news for Luke was that he would miss over a week of school. On his last day in class he did his best to annoy and tease everybody else with his constant reminders of where he was going.

'It'll be deadly. This time tomorrow I'll be in America lapping it up,' boasted Luke. 'You lot will be freezing.'

His teacher, Mr Phelan, by now extremely exasperated with Luke's disruptive attitude, approached him.

'Look Carroll, I'm warning you for the last time. If there's another word out of you I'm going to talk to the principal about cancelling your holiday.'

'But Sir, you can't do that. I was just letting the others know where I'd be in case anyone was looking for me,' replied Luke, trying to sound sincere.

'That's my final warning. I won't say it again,' growled Mr Phelan, pointing his bony finger in Luke's face. 'One more word and you're in big trouble.'

'That shook you,' muttered Fatso Byrne from behind Luke's desk.

By four o'clock Luke had forgotten all about school and cycled home in record time. His mother was putting the final touches to the packing.

'Luke, I want you to have a bath early and be in bed by eight o'clock,' she explained.

'Will you get a life, Mam. Eight o'clock. You wouldn't even be in bed that early if you were really sick,' he pleaded.

'Okay. Have it your own way but we are all getting up at four in the morning,' she shrugged. 'Don't say I didn't warn you.'

Luke's mouth opened wide. 'Four . . . but that's the middle of the night.'

His mother sighed in agreement, 'Tell me about it. I've got to be up too.'

Despite Luke's protests all the family were in bed early but no one slept very well. Eight hours later they were woken by the clanging sound of two alarm clocks. Mr and Mrs Carroll were up instantly but Luke and Barbara had to be dragged red-eyed out of their beds. While their mother made tea and toast, their father packed the luggage into the car. For once Luke was too tired to even moan or mumble a few words. Dead on schedule they left the house at four-forty. With virtually traffic-free roads they drove into the airport car park at five-thirty. Damian and Sticky were already waiting for them when they walked into the departure terminal.

Luke got a sudden burst of energy on spotting his pals. 'How long are you guys here?' he called.

'My dad dropped us off a few minutes ago,' replied Sticky.

'I can't wait,' said Damian, rubbing his hands.

The group joined the queue at the Aer Lingus desk and checked in their luggage. They enjoyed a quick coke and scone in the upstairs café and headed for the security gate.

Mr Carroll hugged them and wished them luck. 'Have a great time . . . and, Luke, no messing, do you hear me?'

'Me, Dad? Never,' cried Luke, putting on his best innocent expression.

They had their boarding passes checked and then put their hand luggage through the security machine. Barbara and Sticky walked through safely. Then came Luke's turn. As he passed through the arched metal detector the alarm sounded.

'Back again, son and empty out your pockets,' instructed the security guard.

Luke's face reddened as he walked backwards. He removed his money belt and emptied the keys and small change out of his pockets. He confidently stepped forward but the alarm sounded again. He bit his bottom lip and felt extremely embarrassed. His mother glared at him. Luke tapped the outside of his jeans's pocket. Then he got an idea. To the amazement of everybody present he went into a handstand. He wriggled himself around. Out of the lining of his jeans fell a magnet and some more coins. His mother looked mortified as the crowd of onlookers smiled and tittered.

'You're impossible, Luke. When will you ever learn?' whispered his mother crossly as she pulled him aside. She was still giving out to him when they boarded the Aer Lingus plane.

Luke remained silent until they were on board. He found this the best method when his mother went on the rampage. He hurried down the aisle and on discovering Row 24 he jumped into the window seat.

'I bag the window seat,' he cried.

Damian wasn't pleased. 'Hey, that's not fair.'

Mrs Carroll winked at Damian as he sat next to Luke. 'Don't worry, it'll be your turn on the next plane.'

Barbara and Sticky sat in the next two seats behind Luke and Damian and Mrs Carroll sat directly behind them.

'This is really deadly. It's the first time I've ever been on a plane,' said a delighted Sticky, as they buckled their seat belts.

'I hope you enjoy it because you're going to be doing a lot of air travel over the next while,' said Mrs Carroll, as the plane took off.

Within fifty minutes they were flying over London and the children spotted familiar landmarks below them.

'Isn't that the Thames?' cried Barbara, pointing to the river directly below them.

'And look at the London Eye . . . it's enormous,' yelled Luke, pointing down to the big wheel.

Sticky was too flabbergasted to even speak. He just stared and said nothing.

Within minutes they had landed at Heathrow Airport – Terminal One. Mrs Carroll consulted her notes and informed the children that they were to transfer to Terminal Four. They walked into the Arrivals building and followed the signs along passageways, escalators and down stairs. Finally they found themselves boarding the Paddington Express, a train which ran underground to their destination. When they arrived at Terminal Four the kids couldn't believe their eyes. The enormous building resembled a shopping centre, with an array of shops and restaurants. They bought a few last minute essentials and had tea and cakes, until it was time to board the plane for the transatlantic flight.

Over the intercom they heard the announcement: 'Flight BA204 for San Francisco is now boarding at Gate 52.'

'That's our plane . . . hurry up . . . we'll be late,' exclaimed Luke charging towards the departure area.

'Don't worry, Luke. They won't leave without us. There

are hundreds of passengers,' smiled his mother.

Making their way to the designated departure gate they watched as young children and invalids were allowed to board the British Airways flight first.

'That's not fair . . . we're kids too,' complained Luke.

His mother's face reddened as people turned to glare at him. 'You're doing it again, Luke. I'll swing for you,' she muttered through clenched teeth. 'Button up and behave yourself.'

Luke lowered his head and said nothing else until they were boarding the plane.

'Look at the size of this baby . . . it's colossal,' said Sticky, his mouth open wide in astonishment.

Damian glanced from side to side. 'It's like a hotel . . . and take a gawk at the enormous screen.'

'I bag the window seat,' said Luke, as he sprang into the seat.

His mother grabbed him by the ear and pulled him up. 'Oh no, you don't. It's Damian's turn this time. You've got a short memory.'

'Oh thanks, Mrs Carroll,' replied Damian, as the two boys exchanged seats.

Luke began to sulk. 'That's not fair, so it's not. This flight's much longer.'

His mother remained firm. 'You should have thought about that earlier. That's what you get for rushing.'

Barbara opened the two packs that were set out on each of the seats. 'Wow, look what we have . . . a blanket . . . and socks . . . and earphones.'

Sticky placed the headset on his head and fiddled with the controls. 'I've got music,' he announced. 'Aagh! It's like the stuff my granny listens to . . . real yackie. Is there

24

no Red Hot Chili Peppers?'

They settled into their seats and fastened their seat belts. Damian and Luke looked out the window attentively as the huge airbus taxied along the runway. They pointed out the planes of several other airlines. Soon they felt the sensation of being forced back into their seats as the plane took off and accelerated up into the clouds. Their big adventure was beginning. The cabin crew walked along the aisles handing out drinks and a menu.

'Food and all. This is better than a holiday,' remarked a delighted Damian.

'And look . . . look, there's two films on as well . . . *Men in Black II* and *Minority Report*,' said Sticky excitedly as he flicked through the in-flight magazine.

Mrs Carroll wasn't looking forward to the ten-hour flight and hoped that the foursome would behave themselves. But she had nothing to worry about. For the remainder of the flight they ate, drank, glanced at magazines, watched the big screen and snoozed.

3

SAN FRANCISCO

Barbara and her mum were looking down on long tracts of desert when there was an announcement over the tannoy system.

'This is the captain. I would just like to inform you that we will be landing in San Francisco in about one hour's time. It is a warm and sunny day there and the temperature is 84°F/29°C. If you want to adjust your watches the time there is twelve-thirty. I hope you all enjoyed the flight and will travel with British Airways again soon.'

With this news Luke sat upright and began peering out the window.

'I wonder is that twelve-thirty night time or day time?' asked Damian.

'You're a right eejit,' snapped Luke. 'Where would you see the sun at half-twelve at night?'

'Oh yeah, I forgot,' replied a sleepy Damian.

'That flight was very short. I thought it was suppose to take ten hours,' said Sticky examining his watch. 'I make it only two hours. Someone's got it wrong.'

Luke prodded him with his finger. 'You're thick, so you are. Your watch has to be put back eight hours. Anyway, you slept most of the time. We ate your ice cream as well.'

Sticky appeared startled. If there were sweets being given out, Sticky was always first in the queue. 'Come off it. I didn't see any ice cream. Is that right, Mrs Carroll?'

'I'm afraid it is. And you have a great loud snore,' she

laughed. 'Hey kids, look! That's the Nevada mountain range.' A short time later she pointed out Lake Tahoe.

Some distance further on Barbara asked, 'Is that Silicon Valley?'

'Looks like it,' replied her mother.

'Isn't that where they have all the computer gear?' remarked Luke.

Sticky was flabbergasted. 'I often heard about these places on the telly but I never thought I'd see them for real. It's like a miracle.'

By the time the 'Fasten seat belts' sign had come on they had organised themselves and were chatting excitedly about everything they would see in San Francisco. Soon the plane was flying low over the sea for its approach to the runway. There was only a slight bump as the plane made a smooth landing.

'Are we really in America now?' asked Sticky with disbelief.

A bleary-eyed Mrs Carroll replied, 'We are indeed. This is San Francisco, California. Welcome to the USA.'

There followed a tiresome fifty minutes as they disembarked, collected their luggage and went through immigration control. With Luke pushing one trolley and Damian the other they headed for the arrivals lounge where a semi-circle of people, some happy, some anxious, waited for the new arrivals. Some of the crowd were holding placards with names scrawled on them. As the glass screens parted the children's eyes darted from face to face as they attempted to spot Todd.

'Luke, over here,' called a familiar voice. Luke scanned the faces and then spotted a smiling Gordon, Todd's minder who had travelled with the young film star to Ireland. Luke hurried towards him.

'Welcome to San Francisco,' said Gordon. 'I hope you'll have an enjoyable time.'

'It's deadly to be here,' replied Luke as Gordon took the trolley from him and they joined the others.

'You remember my mother, my sister, Barbara, and of course Sticky and Damian,' said Luke.

'Hi Gordon,' said Luke's mother. 'It's nice to see you.'

'Likewise, ma'am,' smiled Gordon.

Mrs Carroll and the children followed Gordon out of the airport. It was a warm, sunny day with not a cloud in the sky. Lined up alongside the pavement was a queue of colourful cabs with people of all nationalities scrambling into them.

Gordon led them to a black stretch limo. He opened the boot and began packing in the luggage.

'Would you take a look at that,' remarked Damian as he admired the vehicle. 'At home three cars stuck together wouldn't be that long.'

The rear door of the car opened slightly and a whisper came from inside, 'Hi Luke, how are you?'

Luke instantly recognised the voice. He rushed towards the door and swung it open to see Todd in the back seat.

'Todd . . . it's brill to see you. How are things?' Luke jumped inside and slapped his friend on the arm.

'Cool,' replied the American star. 'Sorry I couldn't wait for you in the airport but I would have been mobbed.'

'Sure, no problem.' Luke was bubbling with excitement and had so many questions to ask. 'It feels like a dream being here. I still can't believe it.'

Todd grinned. 'In a couple of days you'll be used to it. Before you leave I guarantee you'll know San Francisco as well as Bray.'

'I can't wait . . . this is supposed to be one of the best places in the world,' replied Luke.

The remainder of the luggage was packed away and the rest of the group got into the limo. Todd greeted them all enthusiastically, delighted to see them again.

'Now for your first look at the city,' said Gordon as he guided the car away from the side walk.

Mrs Carroll had to pinch herself to check that this was for real. 'I feel like a queen or some pop star . . . a stretch limo,' she mumbled in disbelief.

'But why are the windows dark from the outside?' enquired Sticky.

'For a very good reason. You can't see in from the outside but you can see out,' explained Todd. 'Madonna or Brad Pitt could be in the next limo you see.'

Sticky pushed his face against the glass. 'Oh I like that. You could be doing anything, like picking your nose or scratching yourself, and nobody could see you.'

'Watch this,' called Todd as he pressed a button on a remote control and a screen drew back and revealed a large TV screen.

'A telly in the car. What next?' exclaimed Barbara.

Todd pressed some more buttons to reveal a bar, a stereo system and a fridge from which he gave them all cool drinks.

'Brill, you wouldn't need a house over here. You could live in the car,' remarked a delighted Damian.

Suddenly Luke let out a yell, 'Hey, watch out! You're on the wrong side of the road.'

Gordon and Todd burst into loud laughter. 'You really are dumb, Luke. You're in the States now. We drive on the right hand side,' teased Todd.

Luke lowered his head and blushed. 'Oh yeah, I forgot. I've seen enough films to know.'

As they approached the city Gordon began pointing out landmarks to them. 'If you look up to the left you'll see Twin Peaks. From there you get the view of the whole Bay area.'

'Wasn't there something on the telly with that name?' said Damian.

Todd nodded. 'Sure, you'll spot movie and TV locations all over the city. The *Dirty Harry* movies, some *James Bond*, *Mrs Doubtfire* and *Star Trek* are a few that were made here.'

'It's nearly like Bray,' commented Luke cheekily. 'Films getting made everywhere.'

'Except for the weather,' smiled his mother.

The children's eyes swivelled from side to side as Gordon and Todd gave them the guided tour.

'There's the Bay Bridge. During the '89 earthquake there were a lot of casualties when one of the levels collapsed,' said Gordon as he pointed to the spectacular two-span bridge that stretched across the bay.

'Todd, did you ever see an earthquake?' asked Luke.

Todd smiled. 'Only a small one. We were in the limo and it felt like a strong wind against the car. You feel dizzy as well.'

'Wow,' said Luke excitedly. 'Maybe we'll see one while we're here.'

'God forbid,' muttered his mother. 'I'd be a nervous wreck. Don't even mention the word.'

The limo brought them on the scenic route along the coast where they saw ferries sailing to and from Sausalito and Tiburon. They passed the ferry building and marinas with sailing vessels, yachts, an American navy destroyer and cruise liners.

Luke pointed to an island with a flashing light, which sat in the middle of the bay. 'What's that out there? It looks familiar.'

'Is it Alcatraz?' asked his mother.

'That's it, Mrs Carroll. We'll go there one day. You probably know it from films like *The Rock*,' said Todd.

Luke clicked his fingers, 'That's it! And look at that place . . . with bands . . . and clowns . . . and burger places . . . there's loads of things.'

'That's Pier 39 and Fisherman's Wharf. We'll get there too. Wait till you see the sea lions. You're going to have a busy time,' promised Todd.

'Not half,' said Luke, his eyes wide open. 'We should have come for a month.'

'Look . . . look . . . look . . . there it is,' cried Sticky, unable to get the words out.

'The Golden Gate Bridge, one of the most famous landmarks in the States,' said Gordon as he slowed the limo to give them a better view.

Mrs Carroll was shaking her head in amazement. 'I never thought I'd live to see this day. I've seen so many pictures and postcards of it.'

'And there'll be lots more, Mrs Carroll,' said Todd, pleased that they were all enjoying their first visit to his city.

The limo drove away from the tourist area to Sea Cliff, an exclusive residential district overlooking the sea. Each of the houses was like a mini-mansion with palm trees and exotic plants in the garden. They slowed down outside one house and the electronic gates opened, allowing the limo to drive in slowly.

'This is it. We're home,' announced Todd proudly.

'This is your house? It's gigantic,' said a bewildered Damian as they climbed out of the limo.

Mrs Carroll was overcome. 'Would you believe it?' she mumbled in a trance-like state as she stared at the two-storey cream-coloured house. Around each of the twelve windows there were ornate carvings of Roman gods.

Barbara stood staring at the house. 'It must be worth a bomb.'

Todd pointed to a nearby house. 'Well, Rock View over there was sold a few months ago for eight million.'

'Eight million . . . eight million dollars,' repeated Luke.

While the Irish group were admiring the house and neighbourhood Gordon began unloading the luggage. Moments later the large, ornate hall door opened and Todd's parents came out to greet them. They were both in their early forties with great tans and shining white teeth. They were dressed in white shorts and T-shirts.

Mrs Harper offered her hand to Luke's mother. 'You are most welcome, Mrs Carroll. We've heard so much about you from Todd. You made his stay in Bray such a pleasant one.'

Mrs Carroll shook hands with her. 'Thank you very much, but Todd is such a mannerly, generous boy. The children just hit it off. Please call me Andrea.'

Mrs Harper made the introductions. 'I'm Harriet and this is my husband, Glen.'

Mr Harper stepped forward to shake hands. 'I hope you enjoy your stay with us.'

Mrs Carroll still appeared bewildered. 'You're so kind. I can't believe I'm actually here. It's a trip of a lifetime for the children.'

'Once they and Todd enjoy themselves that's the main thing,' said Mr Harper.

Todd brought the children over to meet his parents. When he introduced Luke Mr Harper winked at him. 'I believe you're a bit of a rogue.'

Luke's face reddened. 'I . . . I . . . '

His mother spoke sternly. 'He was warned to be on his best behaviour. Let's hope he keeps his promise.'

Mr Harper gave an even bigger grin. 'Not at all. Let him be himself. We want them all to enjoy themselves, no restrictions.'

'If you come inside we'll show you to your rooms,' said Mrs Harper as she led them into the house. 'You probably want to shower and unwind.'

They crossed the large lobby with its thick red carpet. There were pillars at either side of it and adorning the walls was a range of photographs, paintings and posters of Todd's films. Overlooking the staircase was a huge stained-glass window. The dining room consisted of one glass wall with a magnificent view out over the Bay.

Todd escorted the three boys to their room. 'This is where you'll be based, guys. Hope you like it.'

'Like it?' yelled Luke. 'It's the biggest bedroom I've ever seen. All the bedrooms in our house put together wouldn't be this big.'

It was like entering wonderland as the three boys explored the enormous bedroom. There were three single beds, a television, a small pool table and a fridge full of ice cream and minerals.

'If I had a room like this I'd never leave it,' said Sticky, moving around the room, touching everything.

Luke lifted his case onto his bed and began unpacking. 'I can't wait to get into my shorts. Is it always this sunny, Todd?'

'No way. When the mist comes down it even blots out the bridge,' said Todd, amused by their reaction. 'Sometimes you can't see it for days.'

'You couldn't ask for any more than this. It's really cool,' said Sticky as he set up the balls on the pool table.

'Listen, I'll leave you guys to it. I've got a couple of things to do. We'll be eating at six,' said Todd as he headed for the door.

Luke sat on the edge of his bed and bounced up and down. 'Sure, Todd, and thanks again for everything. It's deadly.'

'No problem. Glad to have you guys over,' grinned Todd as he shut the door.

Damian spun around in the centre of the room. 'We're really steeped and it's not costing us a thing. I wish ole Breandie in school could see us now. Maybe we should ring him and ask him to send over our ecker.'

'Give it a rest. How can you even joke about it? Don't mention that joint again,' snapped Sticky.

'We'll have to take stacks of photos and really make them sick when we get back. Show them our bedroom . . . and the house . . . and loads with Todd,' cried Luke, becoming more excited by the minute.

Sticky pointed out the window. 'I definitely want one taken of me on the Golden Gate Bridge.'

Barbara and her mother had a slightly smaller but equally attractive room.

'I never thought I'd be inside a house like this, never mind staying in one,' purred Mrs Carroll.

Barbara ran her hand over the curtain and remarked 'Feel that material. It's like silk.'

'I don't know what to wear for dinner,' said Mrs Carroll with a frown. 'I'm sure they'll be dressed to the nines.'

'Don't worry, Mam. You'll be fine,' encouraged Barbara with a smile. 'You always look great.'

Showered and changed, Mrs Carroll went to the boys' room to inspect their dress code. After a few minor adjustments they were presentable and all five headed down to dinner. Todd's mother met them at the end of the stairs and led them into the dining room which overlooked a landscaped garden with palm trees and statues. The large rectangular table was set out for eight people. It reminded Luke of the layout in the posh hotel in Enniskerry.

'Sit wherever you like,' invited Mrs Harper.

Luke was first to sit down. Todd sat beside him and then the rest of them sat around the table.

'I hope you haven't gone to too much bother for us,' said Mrs Carroll apologetically.

Luke hated when his mother went on like this. It was real crawling. He glared at her.

'Not in the least. It's lovely to have you,' said Mrs Harper, unfolding her napkin. 'Todd has been looking forward to your coming for so long.'

Then two girls in maids' uniforms came into the room carrying trays. They placed a seafood salad before each person. Luke turned it over with his fork. He hated fish and salad.

Todd nudged Luke. 'I bet you don't like salad either.'

Luke winked at him. 'Good guess Todd. How did you know?'

Mrs Harper held up her finger. 'Okay boys, we get the

35

message loud and clear. You don't have to eat the salad.'

Mrs Carroll appeared uneasy. 'I'm so sorry after all the trouble you went to. Luke why did . . .?' She stopped suddenly and said no more. She wasn't at home now. It wouldn't be mannerly to keep checking him. In the end only the adults ate the seafood salad. The second course was French onion soup, which everybody enjoyed. The main course was fillet steak and chips.

Todd nudged Luke. 'This is more like it now. Can we have steak and fries every day?'

'I'm sure our guests would soon tire of that at every meal, son,' said Todd's father as he shook salt on his meal.

'I love steak and chips, Mr Harper. Them and Big Macs I could eat all day,' said Luke through a full mouth. 'Just stack them up.'

'I suppose that goes for the rest of you too?' asked Mrs Harper.

All the children nodded.

Mrs Carroll relaxed a little and said, 'It seems that kids have the same likes the world over. I can't get them to eat proper food at home.'

They finished the meal with fresh fruit and ice cream, followed by coffee. As the parents chatted, Luke began to snooze and Damian rubbed his eyes. The adults were amused.

'Luke tries to be a know-it-all and full of energy but underneath he's really only a child,' said his mother as she tried to conceal a yawn.

'Why don't you all go to bed? You must be exhausted after the long journey,' said Mrs Harper in a friendly tone. 'We won't be offended. Please. You'll feel fresh after a good night's sleep.'

36

'Yes, I think I will. I'm sorry but I can't keep my eyes open,' said Barbara.

'Come on children,' said Mrs Harper gently clapping her hands. 'You'll all feel better in bed.'

Without a grumble or complaint all the children quietly left the room and went to bed. Luke's mother thanked the Harpers for a lovely meal and said that she would see them in the morning.

4

EXPLORING

At seven o'clock the next morning Todd tiptoed from his room across the landing to where Luke, Sticky and Damian were staying. He gently knocked on the door. There was no reply. He slipped into the room.

'Come on, you sleepy heads. It's a lovely morning,' said Todd in a loud whisper.

'Ah, go away, there's plenty of time . . . it's too early. Just another few minutes . . . please,' mumbled Luke, half-asleep.

Todd had to prevent himself laughing out loud. 'There's no school today, Luke. Have you forgotten where you are?'

Luke half lifted his head off the pillow. 'What . . . what . . . who's that?'

Todd was greatly amused by the situation. 'Do you know who this is?'

With great effort Luke opened one eye. He almost fell out of the bed when he saw Todd standing in front of him. 'Todd . . . ' He reached out his hand and grabbed Todd's T-shirt. 'Todd . . . you're for real,' he exclaimed.

'I sure am,' smiled Todd. 'Are you like this every morning?'

Luke rubbed his knuckles against his eyes. 'I hate the mornings. I can never get up but this is different . . . I'm in San Francisco . . . yippee,' he cried as he leaped out of bed.

The noise woke Damian and Sticky.

'What's going on?' asked Damian in a weary voice. 'What's all the bloody racket?'

Todd ran to both of their beds and pulled back the covers. 'Up and at it, guys. You've got a lot to see and do.'

'Oh my God,' exclaimed Sticky. 'It's really Todd and I thought it was all a dream.'

Todd stood with his hands on his hips in the centre of the bedroom. 'I know that I played a ghost in one movie but this is no dream. You're here to enjoy yourselves. Take a look out the window and I'll show you.'

The three boys followed Todd to the window where he drew back the blinds. A shaft of light burst into the room. 'What about that?' he said as he pointed towards the Golden Gate Bridge.

They looked in the direction he indicated. The lower section of the red bridge was shrouded in mist with only the top two spans visible.

'Wow, would you take a look at that. It looks like something out of a space film,' said Luke.

As the boys admired the view Todd spoke, 'Get dressed, guys, and we'll head down for breakfast.'

'I won't say no to that,' said Luke, as he hurried to where his clothes lay in a bundle on the floor.

Ten minutes later Luke, Damian and Sticky entered the dining room. Mrs Carroll and Barbara were giving Todd's parents the presents they had brought for them. Mrs Harper was holding up an Aran sweater that Luke's mother had knitted for her. 'It really is magnificent. Look at the intricate needlework. You're very gifted, Andrea.'

'Ah, it's nothing,' said Mrs Carroll modestly.

Todd's father was inspecting a Waterford Glass clock. 'Gee, take a look at the work that's gone into this piece. Those guys must be skilled. We weren't expecting anything like this. You shouldn't have . . . really.'

Mrs Carroll became embarrassed. 'They're only a few small things as a token. We have a few little mementoes for Todd as well.'

Todd quickly tore the paper off the parcel. 'Wow, sweatshirts and T-shirts with Bray and County Wicklow logos. Gee thanks, I think they're cool.'

'Hope you like them. I picked them out,' said Luke as he held a sweatshirt with a picture of Bray Head up to Todd's chest.

Todd cocked his head. 'I love them. Everybody is tired listening to me talking about Bray since I got back.'

'Now Todd is dying to show you guys the sights around the city,' began Mr Harper. 'Usually he gets mobbed and can't go anywhere but he came up with an idea himself. He—'

Todd cut in. 'Let me tell them, Dad. I was wondering if all you guys wouldn't mind wearing the same shorts, T-shirts and baseball caps as me. It's possible nobody might notice me then. What do you think?'

Luke seemed pleased. 'I think that's a deadly idea. We'd look like a football team or something.'

'That's settled then. I've got stacks of everything. Come on up with me and try them on,' said Todd as he headed for the door.

His father called them back. 'Just one thing. You're not going on your own. Gordon's going too.'

Todd seemed disappointed. 'But Dad, I never get—'

Mrs Carroll butted in, 'I'd like to go as well. Otherwise how am I going to see the place?'

Todd's mother nodded in agreement. 'An excellent idea. I hope you like the city.'

'I'll just love it, I know. Even the small part I saw

40

coming in from the airport looked breathtaking,' replied Mrs Carroll.

'You kids go and get ready so,' said Mrs Harper with a wave of her hand.

The children left the room chatting among themselves. They returned minutes later all dressed exactly the same – white shorts, runners, CAL baseball caps, and T-shirts with the Golden Gate Bridge emblazoned across the front. The adults were greatly amused and burst out laughing.

'You look like the terrible five,' remarked Mr Harper.

Todd's mother addressed the children. 'Thank you all for going along with this idea. Todd has pleaded with me to allow you to travel around as normally as possible as he doesn't often get the chance. '

'Sure thing, Mrs Harper,' said Luke. 'We don't mind. And anyway it's not as if anyone knows us over here.'

'Just one piece of advice, guys. Don't make eye contact with anyone. It can be dangerous,' advised Mr Harper.

The children nodded without question.

Todd's mother went on to explain that she had got them bus and cable car passes which would allow them to travel as often as they liked for the duration of their visit. Gordon and Mrs Carroll would stay with them all day.

'Right Todd, you're the guide. Where to first?' asked his father.

Todd grinned. 'That's easy. The sea lions at Fisherman's Wharf. They're fabulous. The guys have to see them.'

'An excellent idea. That's settled. Out to the cars everybody,' instructed Mr Harper as he headed for the door.

'Not so fast,' began Mrs Harper. 'You have to do one important thing before you head off.' She moved towards them with a tube of sun block. She began rubbing the cream into Todd's arms.

'Oh Mom, I can do it,' he said, taking the tube from her. 'How do you expect me to get a tan?'

Mrs Carroll clicked her fingers and rummaged in her bag. 'The very thing I'd completely forgotten about it. We don't want anyone down sick with sunstroke.'

Quickly Luke, Barbara, Sticky and Damian spread a coating of sun block on their faces, arms and legs, then charged through the house and out to the two cars. Mrs Carroll joined them and Mr Harper and Gordon drove them up and down the hilly streets to Fisherman's Wharf.

Once there, Mr Harper dropped them off. 'Okay, you guys. I'm off. I've got a meeting. Have a great time. See you later,' he said with a smile and wave.

Gordon parked the car and the seven of them set off to explore. Fisherman's Wharf and Pier 39 were bustling areas crowded with bronzed tourists of all nationalities wandering around dressed in T-shirts and shorts. Todd brought them onto Pier 39, a lively waterfront shopping and dining centre. Throughout the two-level complex there was a delightful array of shops, boutiques and numerous seafood restaurants. Lots of people were sitting around drinking large containers of coffee and cold drinks. Anchored alongside the pier was the fishing fleet and the USS *Pampanito*, a World War Two submarine.

'Boy, would you look at her. An old granny on rollerblades,' cried Luke. They all turned to stare as a middle-aged woman in shorts, T-shirt and a crash helmet whizzed by them.

'In San Francisco she's normal. Wait till you see some of the more unusual sights,' grinned Todd. 'Follow me.' He began running, zig-zagging in and out between the people, until he reached the end of the pier. The others followed him as quickly as they could. Mrs Carroll and Gordon walked at a more leisurely pace. Todd leaned over the rail and glanced down into the water. 'Take a look at that,' he said with glee. 'Isn't that some sight?'

They all stopped beside him and gazed downwards. There lying below them on floating docks were hundreds of large sea lions basking in the sun. Some dipped in and out of the water.

Luke, Sticky and Damian opened their mouths in astonishment. Luke reached into his pocket for the remains of a toffee bar and was about to throw it in when Todd tipped him on the arm and pointed to a sign, which read 'Do not feed the sea lions.' Luke put the toffee away.

'There must be hundreds of them,' exclaimed Sticky.

Damian scoffed, 'Sure beats the one or two we have in Dublin Zoo.'

'This colony of sea lions arrives back here every year,' said Gordon as he took an informal photograph of the children.

'This is one of my favourite places. I love coming here,' said Todd, 'but usually some kid spots me and there's a big panic and we have to leave in a hurry.'

'So far so good today,' said Luke with a wink.

They remained watching the antics of the sea lions for a while more. Then Todd brought them to visit some of the other attractions in the area including a turbo ride, an antique two-storey carousel, the Cinemax Theatre featuring *The Great San Francisco Adventure* and various amusement arcades.

'And we thought the ones in Bray were deadly,' said

Luke as they sat in the shade on Pier 39.

'I still like your Star Amusements and the bowling alley in Bray,' said Todd with fond memories.

'Quick, here comes a fishing boat,' cried Sticky as he moved over to the rail. They all watched attentively as the fishermen began unloading crates of shrimp, oysters and lobster. Some still wriggled about in the crates.

'Wait till you see what's in here,' said Todd as they entered Under Water World.

The display of sea creatures was fantastic. All the children were intrigued by the sharks in the aquarium, except Damian, who backed away towards the door. 'No way, they're too close for my liking.'

'You're a right babby. You should have brought your mammy with you,' teased Sticky.

5

CHINATOWN

For the next hour Todd brought his visitors along the quay, where they watched jugglers, mime artists and street performers.

'Anybody hungry?' asked Gordon, glancing at his watch.

'I'm starving,' cried Luke.

'And me,' added Sticky. 'My stomach's rumbling.'

Todd laughed. 'I see nothing's changed, Sticky. One thing's for sure you won't be stuck for somewhere to eat here.'

Gordon clapped his hands. 'Listen up lads. You can either go into a restaurant here or get a picnic in Levi Park. What's the verdict?'

'I'm all for a picnic. We never get the weather for one at home,' said Luke without hesitation.

Gordon nodded at Mrs Carroll. 'Sounds good to me. I've nearly forgotten what a picnic tastes like,' she smiled.

They were all in agreement so the adults found a delicatessen and bought the food. The group then sat in a shaded spot in the park. There was a delicious mix of food including barbecued ribs, mixed salads, ice cream and an assortment of soft drinks. A jazz band played on a small stage in the centre of an ornate pond.

'Oh boy, this is the life. Sure beats eating cheese sambos in the school yard. I'd give anything to do this every day,' said Luke as he stretched out on the grass.

His mother couldn't help laughing. 'Cheese singles sandwiches suit you fine at home. You kick up a right fuss when you forget them the odd time. But if you work harder in school and get into college, you might be able to get a good job and afford to live out here.'

'Ah Mam, get a life. Don't take the good out of it and start that old tripe again,' moaned Luke. 'I don't want to hear another word about school.'

Barbara lay on the grass with her eyes closed. 'If the girls could only see me now. They'd do their nut.'

Todd smiled at her. 'I'd say they'd be rightly jealous. Hey, why don't we take some more photos, Gordon? Day Two in San Francisco?'

'A good idea,' answered his minder as he opened the camera hanging around his neck.

This was the cue for the others to take out their cameras also. They all took a variety of photographs with different people. Then they sat down to chat.

Todd leaped to his feet. 'Listen, we're wasting time. I've got an idea. Follow me,' he called, as he headed for the gate. They all sprang to their feet and half-ran after him.

'Where to?' asked Gordon.

'Coit Tower,' Todd shouted over his shoulder.

Gordon's big white teeth showed when he smiled. 'You're cruel, Todd. I hope they like steps. If not, they'll be crippled.'

'Are there many steps?' asked Luke. 'I love heights. The higher the better.'

Todd led them from the park up the hundreds of steps to one of the most famous landmarks in San Francisco – Coit Tower. In 1933 the 95-metre tower was built on top of Telegraph Hill.

'Let's go all the way up,' suggested Todd as he led the group into the small lift. It brought them to the top of the needle-shaped tower.

Mrs Carroll was overcome with the view. 'Would you believe that,' she exclaimed. 'You can see the two bridges and the entire city. It's breathtaking. Your father would love this, Barbara.' While his mother was enjoying the scenery Luke spotted a way of having some fun. Directly beneath him, at the base of the tower a group of Japanese tourists were posing for a photograph. Checking to see that nobody was watching Luke took a chunk of toffee from his pocket. He rolled it around in his mouth and took it out feeling nice and sticky. He leaned over the rail, took aim and dropped the toffee down onto a Japanese woman's head. He heard a screech from below and quickly drew back his head.

Luke was smirking when Todd approached him. 'What have you been up to?' asked the American.

'Me . . . nothing,' replied Luke, trying to be casual. 'Well, I may have dropped a toffee on that Japanese lady's head!' He laughed at the surprised look on Todd's face.

'OK, everybody,' said Todd. 'Time to move along.'

Luke's mother was so absorbed in the scenery that she didn't want to leave. 'Oh I suppose we better.'

Luke led them smartly towards the lift. When the doors opened the group of Japanese stepped out, glaring at Mrs Carroll and the children. Luke and Todd quickly entered the lift, followed by the others; the doors closed and it went down.

'They didn't at all look friendly,' remarked Mrs Carroll.

Luke shrugged. 'They're probably exhausted climbing all the hills in the heat.'

Todd covered his mouth with his hand to conceal his amusement.

Mrs Carroll eyed them suspiciously. 'Luke Carroll, I hope you haven't been up to any of your tricks? I'll be keeping my eye on you.'

'Ah Mam, don't start. You know me better than that. You never trust me,' said Luke, in his most sincere voice.

When they reached the lobby they spent some time admiring the huge murals depicting life in California in the 1930s. Todd, sensing Luke's desire to move on before the Japanese reappeared, announced that there was lots more still to see. He led them down the steep incline of Telegraph Hill, then darting along Lombard Street he climbed up another steep hill. The others, growing red-faced and more tired by the minute, trailed further behind him.

'Would you ever slow down, Todd,' cried a breathless Luke, as he tried to keep up. 'You might be in training for the next Olympics, but we're not.'

Finally Todd stopped and pointed. 'It's worth the climb. Take a look at this. Bet you haven't got anything like that in Bray.'

Panting and breathless, the rest of the group finally caught up. They found themselves overlooking the beginning of the zigzag that is the Crookedest Street in the World. It was the most unusual street they had ever seen. It comprised of a series of short, sharp, hairpin turns between Hyde and Leavenworth with small hedges and plants dividing the street.

Damian stood on a high wall and called out, 'I remember seeing this street in loads of films.'

'Why did anyone go and build a stupid street like that?'

enquired Sticky. 'Wouldn't it be simpler to make it straight.'

Gordon provided the explanation. 'Well in the 1920s they had to build it like that so that transport could get down.'

While they were admiring the street there was the sound of a bell and a clanging noise. They turned to see a cable car approaching with people standing on platforms on either side.

'Is that a real cable car?' asked Barbara in amazement.

'Sure is,' responded Todd, running towards it. 'And if we're lucky we can get on it in time.'

Mrs Carroll looked concerned, 'But it's full . . . it could be dangerous.'

About ten people hopped off the cable car at the junction. Immediately Todd stepped onto the platform and held onto the bar. The others stood staring at him.

'Come on. Get on quickly . . . before it moves,' yelled Todd.

Luke and the children were first on. Gordon took Mrs Carroll by the arm and assisted her. She looked nervous as she clutched the rail with both hands.

'Man, this is deadly. This is what I love,' yelled Luke as he waved at passers-by.

'Stand clear everybody,' called the jovial driver. He was in a standing position operating a large lever. He released the brake and the cable car moved off.

Barbara, a little unsure at first, was beginning to enjoy herself. 'How long have the cable cars being running? They seem a bit ancient.'

'About 125 years,' explained Gordon, 'but they got completely renovated around 1984. I haven't been on one in years. It's mostly for the tourists.'

'You mean they'd fall for anything,' laughed Mrs Carroll, relaxing a little.

As they came down a steep hill Luke saw something he couldn't resist. A tall man, wearing a stetson was standing at the edge of the sidewalk. As the cable car drew level, Luke stretched out his hand and flicked the man's hat off. It blew down the street. The man leaped onto the street and waved his fist after him.

'You're some guy, Luke,' smiled Todd. 'You never miss a chance.'

Luke glanced over his shoulder and was pleased to see his mother and Gordon were looking in the opposite direction.

'Look out, guys. We're going to be sandwiched,' cried Sticky as another cable car approached from the opposite direction.

'This should be fun,' laughed Todd as the two cable cars passed within a metre of each other.

'Mind your bum, Barbara. It might get sliced off,' jeered Damian.

She stuck her tongue out. 'It would be better if it sliced off your tongue. That wouldn't be any loss.'

Todd spoke loudly over the noise. 'Get ready everybody. We're getting off at the next stop.'

Mrs Carroll spoke to Gordon. 'Where are we going now?'

He smiled. 'Beats me. Let's just stay with them.'

They all got off the cable car at the Cable Car Museum. Todd walked ahead of them at a fast pace and turned into Chinatown.

'Wow,' said Luke. 'This is different.'

Chinatown was a fascinating area of the city. It was home to one of North America's largest Chinese communities. The area of sixteen square blocks was entered at Bush Street through the imposing Dragon Gate, a huge ornate gateway, which was a gift to San Francisco from the Republic of Taiwan. The narrow, crowded streets were adorned with banners, flags and bunting. Restaurants, craftshops and trading companies offered a variety of colourful merchandise – silk, jade, artefacts and oriental antiques – which were all displayed together.

Sticky looked bewildered as he examined the faces closely. 'Are we still in America? All I can see are Chinese. It's like the take-away in Bray.'

'What do you expect, you eejit? This is Chinatown. All the people and shops are Chinese,' replied Barbara as she stopped to admire some silk scarves.

Todd led them up a side street. 'It's better up here. Down there is where all the tourists go.'

Mrs Carroll seemed confused, 'But we are tourists.'

'But this is where the Chinese do all their shopping,' explained Todd as they entered a large outdoor food market with an array of fruit, vegetables, fish and fowl from the Orient.

'Wow, would you take a gawk at that . . . look at the size of the melons. They're about ten times the size of the ones at home,' said Damian as he stared at the stalls.

Mrs Carroll was quick to realise that all the stall holders and customers were speaking their own language. She was fascinated as she wandered through the stalls admiring the merchandise.

'Anybody want to buy souvenirs?' asked Todd, as he

brought them into a large craft shop which sold mementoes of the city, along with silk scarves and kimonos. Browsing through the display stands, Luke became interested in a collection of dragons. They ranged from about fifty centimetres to a metre in length. Having examined one closely he noticed Sticky kneeling on the floor glancing at a book. Luke couldn't resist this great opportunity. He sneaked up behind Sticky and, placing the dragon on his head, cried out, 'Ah . . . he's got you.'

A frightened Sticky sprang to his feet and exclaimed, 'What . . . what . . . is it?' He knocked the dragon out of Luke's hand. It crashed onto the floor and shattered. Within seconds they were quickly surrounded by customers as well as Todd, Barbara, Damian, Mrs Carroll and an angry shopkeeper. The owner, his brow furrowed, waved his arms about wildly and shouted in Chinese.

Luke put on his innocent expression. 'It was an accident. It wasn't my fault. I didn't mean . . .'

His mother grabbed him by the arm. 'Not another word,' she growled through gritted teeth. 'Trust you to ruin the holiday, you little pup. You always push your luck.'

Luke's face was reddening more and more by the second. He lowered his head and nibbled his lower lip while the owner became hysterical and began making gestures indicating that he wanted to be paid for the damage.

Luke's mother spoke sternly. 'You'd better pay up. You're responsible. If you don't, he'll call the police.'

Luke hung his head lower and dug his hands into the waistband of his shorts. 'But it . . . ' he began.

His mother held up her finger. 'Now,' she said in a firm voice. Reluctantly Luke opened his money belt. He took out his folded notes. The owner snapped the bundle from him and peeled off twenty-five dollars. Luke's mouth opened wide. He was dumbfounded and couldn't say anything. The Chinese man shoved the remainder of the notes abruptly back into Luke's hand and then stooped to pick up the broken pieces.

Mrs Carroll sighed with a mixture of frustration and embarrassment. 'We'd better go before there's any more damage done.' She swiftly led the group out of the shop. Luke stood against the window as his mother laced into him. She didn't give him an opportunity to respond. For the remainder of the day Luke was on his best behaviour as they strolled around Chinatown buying some postcards and small gifts. His mother remained directly behind him with a face like thunder.

In the late afternoon they all returned to Todd's house. Luke's mother pulled him aside and spoke firmly to him again. 'You were warned about your messing. Let that be the last of it. Can you imagine what would happen if you broke something here in the house? The cost to replace it. We'd be paying for it for years.'

Luke tried to put up a defence. 'But Mam, it was an accident. I only broke a dragon and it wasn't even that realistic. Loads of things get broken at home. It's not the end of the world. I remember even you breaking things.'

His mother scowled and waved her finger at him. 'Don't start, Luke. I'm warning you. Once more and you're going to be grounded.'

Luke didn't reply and went into a sulk for a while. He wasn't happy with the prospect of his mother looking over his shoulder for the rest of the holiday.

They were all famished after their busy day but there was still half an hour to kill before dinner so Todd brought the children out to meet Old Ben, the gardener. The elderley man knelt on a rubber mat, trowel in hand, weeding the rockery. As they approached him he sat back on his haunches and smiled through his broken teeth.

'The visitors from Ireland. You're welcome,' he chuckled as he rubbed his dirty hands in his overall. 'Excuse the hands.'

Todd quickly introduced them. 'This is their first time over here. You must tell them about your other job,' he said with a quick wink to the gardener.

'Have you been out to Alcatraz yet?' asked Old Ben.

Luke shook his head. 'No.'

Old Ben stroked his grey stubble with a wrinkled hand. 'You have a treat in store. During my time on Alcatraz we had many Irish there. I knew them all. Hard men they were.'

Luke's eyes widened. 'You were on Alcatraz?'

'Sure was. Spent over twenty years there,' he said thoughtfully.

The children all stared at him in awe. They weren't sure whether they should admire him or be scared of him. Finally Sticky asked him, 'Did you know many famous prisoners?'

'Sure did. I think the most famous one I knew was old man Stroud, the Birdman of Alcatraz. I would bring him birdseed for his dozens of birds. It was some sight,' he said, recalling the memories.

Barbara stared at him in disbelief. 'What is it really like out there?'

He shook his head. 'It's a spooky place. They say that the ghosts of Al Capone, Machine Gun Kelly and other criminals prowl the cell block at night. God look sideways on anyone who crosses their path. I wouldn't stay overnight there for a million dollars. No siree. Even today it's a scary place.'

They all wanted to know what crime Old Ben had committed. Finally Luke picked up the courage to ask him. 'What . . . what did you do?'

'Gardening.'

Luke was confused. 'No, I mean why did they send you there?'

'Because I was a good gardener,' smiled the old man.

Todd had to hold his sides, he was laughing so much. 'Old Ben wasn't a prisoner. He was a gardener out there for over twenty years before he came here. You fell for it.'

The children began giggling. 'You're desperate! But did you really see the prisoners?'

Old Ben nodded. 'I saw them all, shackled hands and feet coming in on the ferries. I never want to set foot on The Rock again. It holds too many bad memories. Those guys could get the smells and hears the sounds of the city but couldn't get near it.'

'Don't put them off, Old Ben. We're going out there later in the week,' explained Todd.

6
THE CHASE

Early the next morning Luke was glad to see Todd arriving in his room. He immediately sat upright in his bed.

'Listen Todd, have you got any ideas about losing my mother today? She's doing my head in. We'll have to get rid of her,' said Luke, not sounding too happy.

Sticky raised his head above the covers. 'Yeah, she's a right pain. She sounds worse than my ma does when she's in bad form. "Don't do this and don't do that."'

Todd burst out laughing. 'You guys don't know how well off you are. I always have a minder or my parents with me everywhere. I'd love to swop places.'

'But then you're a big star,' mumbled Damian. 'You're famous. Everybody knows you.'

'True, I suppose. What do you want me to do?' asked Todd, sitting on the edge of Luke's bed.

Luke screwed up his face. 'I'm not sure but there must be some way we can accidentally lose them.'

Todd scratched his head. 'Emm, leave it with me . . . I'm sure I can work something out.'

Luke gave him a friendly punch on the arm. 'I knew we could rely on you. Good old Todd.'

The children and the parents all sat down to a breakfast of juice, cereal, toast and tea.

'And where is the tour guide going to bring his group today?' asked Mr Harper.

Todd emptied his mouth before speaking. 'I was thinking about Union Square, F.A.O. Swartz, Macys and thereabout.'

His father nodded his agreement. 'A good choice. I'm sure Mrs Carroll will be pleased with the shops.'

Mrs Carroll smiled. 'Don't worry about me. This holiday is for the children. Once they're having a good time, that's the main thing.'

'Oh great, I love to hear that,' muttered Luke, rubbing his hands together.

His mother gave him one of her famous stares. He decided not to push it and said nothing more. After breakfast Todd suggested taking the MUNI, the city bus service, into the city centre. After some discussion it was agreed that Gordon and Mrs Carroll would again accompany the children.

They disembarked from the bus close to the classy St Francis Hotel at Union Square in the heart of the city. The square centred around a manicured park which had a naval monument topped with a bronze Goddess of Victory. The square was surrounded by fashionable stores and hotels. As they walked through the square Gordon pointed towards a shop. 'Do you remember the Hitchcock film *The Birds*? Well, the opening scenes were shot over there.'

'That was a real scary film,' said Damian with a shudder.

'You have to see this shop. It's incredible,' said Todd bringing them into F.A.O. Swartz, a large toy shop.

Inside the front door there was a huge mound of teddy bears from ceiling to floor. Barbara made straight for them. She picked up a cuddly teddy and brushed it against her cheek.

Todd crossed over to the stairs. 'Wait till you see what's up here.'

'Wow, *Star Wars*. They've got characters from all the films,' cried Sticky as he passed a stand.

'I'll show you my favourite toy,' said Todd, bouncing up the stairs to the top floor. He took them to a large keyboard lying on the floor. He stepped lightly onto the keys and began tapping out the notes of *Singing in the Rain*. 'Do you recognise that?'

'Oh, I know it,' said Barbara. 'What's this it is? Emm, is it *Singing in the Rain*?'

'Yeah, the very thing. Anybody want to try?' asked Todd, stepping aside.

'I'll give it a bash,' volunteered Barbara. 'I play the piano a bit. I'm not great.'

'The same idea. Just pick out the notes,' explained Todd.

Barbara began playing *Three Blind Mice*.

While the others were amusing themselves with the keyboard Luke drifted away to explore on his own. He soon discovered an enormous Lego display in the shape of a skyscraper, consisting of hundreds of pieces. With a mischievous glint in his eye Luke ran his tongue over his bottom lip. He wondered how big a mess it would make if it collapsed. Much as he would like to see it shatter he wasn't going to be caught again. Then he had an idea. He noticed that the display was supported by a wooden frame. He glanced around to make sure that nobody was watching him and, bit by bit, he manoeuvred the skyscraper off the frame and left it balancing on the edge of the shelf. On noticing two small children approaching, he casually moved away from the stand. He picked up a Halloween mask and tried it on.

Behind him, he heard one of the children cry out, 'Oh Mommy, look at the Lego.' There followed an almighty crash and a scream from the children. Their mother tried to comfort them as the Lego lay in hundreds of small pieces at their feet. Shop assistants dashed to the scene as Mrs Carroll, Gordon and the other children rushed up to investigate the racket.

'You see, anybody can let things fall,' said Luke smugly to his mother.

'Why do I have a suspicion that you could be behind it?' said Mrs Carroll with a puzzled expression.

'Oh that's typical. You try to blame me for everything. Even something another kid did,' he snapped as he walked away. He had won this round.

They remained in the toy shop for a while more before moving on. As they crossed to nearby Macys Department Store Todd whispered to Luke, 'We should be able to lose the adults in here. Are you still on?'

'Not half. I can't wait. My mother's at it again,' replied Luke, relishing the idea of being rid of her.

Leisurely they wandered around the store until Todd suggested to everyone, 'Why don't we split up and we can look at different things? We can meet back at the main door in half an hour.'

'I'm game for that,' said Barbara.

'Me too,' chorused Sticky and Damian.

Mrs Carroll glanced at Gordon. He shrugged.

'Sure, why not? So long as you're not up to any of your stunts,' she said. 'I know you too well. But I could do with a peek into the lady's department.'

'You make sure you stay with the other children, Todd,' instructed Gordon.

'Don't worry, Boss. I won't leave them. That's a promise,' smiled Todd.

'Okay, we'll see you all back at the main door in say . . . forty minutes,' said Mrs Carroll checking her watch.

When Gordon and Mrs Carroll were out of range Luke and Todd gathered the others together. 'We're going to shake the oldies and do our own thing,' explained Luke.

Barbara became annoyed. 'Are you mad or something? Mam will do her nut. We don't know anywhere here.'

Luke turned his back on her and muttered, 'We're off anyway. You can stay here if you want. I don't care.'

'We'll head out this door,' said Todd, running up the stairs and out into a side street.

When the boys reached the street they discovered that Barbara was with them. 'Have you changed your mind, Barbara?' asked Todd with a smile.

She frowned, 'I might as well if you're all going.'

'Great. We're all together. Let's move out of this area before they see us,' said Todd quickly crossing the street and turning into an alleyway. This brought them into Market Street.

'By the way, south of Market is the badlands. Don't ever go down there,' explained Todd.

'Hey! Is that one of the famous Starbucks coffee shops?' asked Sticky as he spotted the name.

'It sure is. Fancy giving it a try?' asked Todd, not waiting for an answer but heading towards the coffee shop.

They all agreed and followed Todd inside, where they sat on high stools around a circular table. When the waitress approached them with a menu Todd ordered five cappuccinos.

Sticky was puzzled. 'What's cappuccino? I only drink

coffee.'

Luke rapped him on the knuckles with a spoon. 'Do you know nothing? It is coffee. It's really frothy with chocolate on top.'

'Oh, I didn't know,' replied Sticky, his cheeks turning pink.

While the others chatted, Damian stared intently out the window. Noticing his frown Todd enquired, 'Are you okay, Damian?'

He replied in a strange, hushed voice, 'Am I imagining things or is that guy in the jeep over there wearing a mask?' He pointed to a jeep parked in the opposite alleyway. They all turned in the direction he indicated.

Luke's brow furrowed, 'I think you're right.'

'Yeah, it looks like a balaclava,' added Barbara. 'Shouldn't we tell someone?' she suggested as she pressed her nose closer to the window.

'It's probably only somebody going to a party. You know, like Halloween or that,' said Damian.

'At this hour of the morning. Are you daft?' Barbara snapped.

Luke nibbled his lowered lip as he thought and then said, 'Let's have a dekko. Maybe we can do something ourselves.'

Sticky seemed nervous. 'Are you crazy? That could be dangerous. He might have a knife or something.'

'What are you like? You're afraid of your own shadow. Let's go and have a closer look. We might see a bit of action,' snapped Luke as he pushed Sticky aside and made for the door.

'Why not?' said Todd, following him out.

After some hesitation the others trailed behind. Luke led

them to a telephone at the side of the street. He picked up the receiver and pretended to be using it.

'Are you phoning the cops?' asked Todd.

'No, just pretending. We can see him better from here. Just wait,' said Luke becoming excited. 'Don't look towards him.'

Meanwhile inside the coffee shop the waitress returned to their table with the five cappuccinos. She was surprised to see that the children were not there. She checked the restrooms but they had disappeared.

Nervously the children clustered around the phone, throwing an occasional glance towards the man with the mask.

Damian was scared. 'Can we go now? I heard that the baddies over here shoot people just for looking at them. Come on, let's blow.'

'Give it a rest, will you. I was dying to see something like this. Beats shopping any day,' said Luke in a loud whisper. He licked his lips with growing excitement.

There was a sudden yell from Todd, 'Look, here comes another guy running . . . he's wearing a mask too . . . he has a bag or something in his hand . . . and he's heading for the jeep.'

'They must be real crooks . . . they've robbed somewhere,' cried Barbara.

Luke clasped his hand over her mouth. 'Keep it down before somebody hears you. You don't want to spoil it.'

They watched anxiously as the second crook jumped into the passenger seat of the jeep. An older man, in shirt sleeves, came out of a door further down the alley and ran towards them, shouting and waving his arms. The jeep was still parked, noisily revving. The man drew closer to the jeep as the two masked men leaped out. They were agitated and the tall crook with the bag was shouting at the plump one, obviously the driver. When the older man drew level with the jeep he attempted to grab the tall crook with the bag.

Luke bit his knuckle. 'Oh, there's going to be a punch up. I can't wait.'

The tall crook swung around and hit the man hard on the side of the head. The older man staggered back clutching his head before falling to the ground.

'They're after killing him,' screamed Barbara.

'No, they didn't. It was only a little bang. Keep it down,' said Luke, now really fired up.

'This is incredible. I never saw a robbery before,' said Todd, hopping around with excitement.

While the children were talking the two men slammed the jeep doors closed and began running back down the alley.

'Are you ready? Let's get after them,' cried Luke as he darted across the street.

Todd immediately took off after him. Reluctantly the others followed. Cars braked and horns blew as the children ran across in front of the traffic. By the time they had reached the stalled jeep the crooks had gone around the corner. The older man was lying moaning on the ground with blood trickling from his head. A group of people were gathering around him while a young woman held a cell phone to her ear. Presumably she had dialled 911 for an ambulance. Seeing that the injured man was being looked after, Luke and Todd broke into a sprint and reached the end of the alley. Luke threw himself flat against the wall and peeped around the corner. In the distance he could see the two men in their black T-shirts, masks removed, half-running, half-walking along the street.

Luke waved the others on. 'Quick, they're getting away. Let's follow them.'

By now even Todd was unsure and appeared uneasy. 'Is it safe, Luke? They're tough guys. Even if we caught up with them what would we do?'

Luke shrugged. 'I haven't got a clue. But this is like the movies. We'll never get another chance like this again. We'll be kicking ourselves if we don't follow them.'

Todd was silent for a second but then took off down the street after the crooks. 'What are you waiting for?' he called back.

7
ALCATRAZ

Luke and the others had to run fast to keep up with Todd. The crooks were tiring and slowing down. From time to time they glanced over their shoulders but the children were alert and slowed to a walk when this happened.

'We're not going to keep chasing them, are we?' asked a weary Sticky. 'This is stupid.'

'Why not? I think it's deadly. This is what I've been waiting for,' cried Luke.

'This is cool. It's like being in a movie for real,' said Todd, running faster.

Damian was beginning to pant. 'But they could run for ever. I'm knackered already. Can we not stop? We've to go all the way back, remember.'

'These guys are ancient. We'll be well able to keep up with them. They'll have to stop soon,' said Todd, as he darted in and out between the pedestrians.

The two crooks raced into the middle of the road and towards a cable car.

'Hey, look . . . they're going to jump on that cable car. If they do, we'll lose them,' yelled Luke.

The crooks increased their speed and with a daring leap they sprang onto the platform on the cable car. The fat guy stumbled. The tall guy dragged him on by the arm. The children watched anxiously as the cable car moved away.

'Hell, we've lost them now. It was good while it lasted,'

said Sticky in a disappointed tone.

'No way, we're not finished yet,' cried Todd, as he waved at a passing cab.

The yellow cab did a U-turn and came to a halt in front of them. The bald taxi driver rolled down his window and called out to them, 'Where to, kids?'

'Follow that cable car,' instructed Todd with urgency in his voice.

The cab driver made a funny face. 'Are you kidding? Is this for real?'

Todd thought fast. 'Eh . . . eh . . . my mom's on it. We have to catch up with her. We're lost.'

'If that's the case, hop in. We'll soon catch her,' said the cab driver earnestly. The children quickly dived into the cab. Todd sat beside the driver. With a screech of brakes the car took off and sped up the hill in pursuit of the cable car.

The cab driver kept glancing towards Todd. 'Do you know who you're the image of? I'd swear you were that young film star, what's his name? Harper, yeah, Todd Harper.'

Todd blushed and laughed. He spoke in a fake Irish accent. 'Sure I know. Every day dozens of people ask me the same question. I wish I had half his money. Sorry to disappoint you, though. I come from Bray in Ireland. Ever heard of the place?'

The cab driver shook his head. 'Na. It doesn't ring a bell. But sure as hell you look his double. I would have put a week's takings on it.'

As the cab followed closely behind the cable car the children kept watch on both sides to make sure that the crooks wouldn't slip off. Suddenly the cable car slowed down. The tall crook jumped off in front of oncoming traffic. A Cadillac blasted its horn. The fat crook followed and headed in the same direction.

'Let's get off here. That's him . . . I mean her,' Todd yelled at the cab driver.

The driver brought the car to an abrupt halt in the centre of the street. He stared after the two crooks in amazement. 'But I thought you said you wanted to catch up with your mother . . . they're guys.'

Todd opened the cab door and winked at him, 'I know. She's a bit funny that way . . . you know.' Todd shoved ten dollars into his hand and sprang out of the car. The other children quickly followed him, tittering and giggling as the cab driver sat with a puzzled expression, scratching his bald scalp.

Meanwhile the crooks were heading towards Fisherman's Wharf where they pushed and barged their way through the tourists strolling on the seafront. The children were following close behind when suddenly an elderly, homeless man pushed his shopping trolley out in front of them. Todd ploughed into the man, sending him sprawling, while Luke upended the trolley, scattering the man's humble belongings all over the ground. Luke and Todd quickly picked themselves up and both bent down to assist the old man to his feet.

'I'm really sorry. I didn't mean it,' said Todd, trying not to inhale the old man's pungent smell.

Luke began straightening the trolley and replacing its contents: a shabby and threadbare blanket, cans of food and beer, old newspapers and sundry pieces of delph and cutlery.

'You lot keep after them,' yelled Luke at the other

hesitant children. They continued to run.

'Don't worry, guys. No harm done. You didn't mean it,' muttered the old man through his gummy mouth.

'Sorry again,' said Todd, shoving twenty dollars into his dirty hand. Then he and Luke took off after the others.

'This is great crack. I hope it never ends,' said Luke with a wide grin as he and Todd caught up with the others.

Suddenly Sticky called out, 'Look, there's a squad car . . . it's the gardaí. Call them . . . quick. They'll nab them.'

'Never mind them, Sticky, let's nab the crooks ourselves,' shouted Todd. 'And by the way, they're called cops over here and they all carry guns.'

'What do you mean we'll nab them? They're grown men. Sure they'll make mincemeat out of us if we get near them,' said Sticky, sounding worried.

Barbara frowned as Todd drew level with her. 'I hope these guys we're chasing haven't got guns.'

Todd, jogging at a steady pace, turned towards her and said,' Lots of people have guns over here. Even my dad has one.'

'He has?' exclaimed Luke.

'Shush everybody . . . they're stopping,' cried Damian, coming to a halt behind a pillar at Pier 39.

The other children piled up behind him. Cautiously they peered around the corner. For the first time they got a close view of the men. The taller man, still clutching the bag, nervously shuffled from foot to foot. He had yellow, spiky hair and a pinched, mean face. The second man had beady eyes, a bullet-shaped, shaven head and a jagged scar running across his right cheek. He was overweight and had bandy legs. He had run with a peculiar waddle and now his legs looked as though they would buckle under his weight.

The tall man moved to a telephone kiosk and dialled a number. After a few minutes he slammed down the receiver and marched back to his partner and dug him threateningly in the chest with his finger. He then shoved the bag at him and approached the hatch of the Blue and Gold Fleet booking office where he bought two tickets. As soon as the coast was clear Todd rushed up to the hatch and spoke to the attendant.

'What's he at?' enquired Sticky.

Before anyone had replied Todd signalled them on. They quickly gathered around him as he handed each of them a ticket. 'They've bought tickets for the ferry to Alcatraz. And we're going out there too.'

Sticky's mouth opened wide in astonishment, 'We're going out to the prison . . . after those crooks . . . are you mad or stupid or what?'

Luke pushed him aside. 'Stay here if you want to . . . you wimp. We're going. No way am I missing this. I'd gladly hand over my pocket money for the next five years.'

Todd led them down the pier and they watched as the two crooks boarded the ferry. Cautiously the children followed them and held back until they discovered where the two men were sitting. The crooks sat beside a window on the inside deck. The children, their faces turned away from them, continued on up to the top deck which was crowded with tourists.

Before long the children were enjoying the warm sun under a cloudless sky. They leaned over the rail as Todd pointed out the landmarks – the Pyramid Building, Coit Tower and Twin Peaks. There was a roar of the engine as the ferry reversed out of its berth. It picked up speed as it began the short journey out to the middle of the bay to

Alcatraz. There was a panoramic view of the Golden Gate Bridge to the left, the Bay Bridge to the right and the tiered white buildings of Sausalito and Tiburon ahead of them. The bay was crowded with yachts, ferries, cruisers and an oil tanker steaming in from the Pacific Ocean.

'Line up against the rail,' instructed Todd, as he removed the cover from his camera. 'This will make a fantastic shot.'

Barbara screwed up her face. 'Damn it, I'm sorry I didn't bring mine.'

'What happens if the guys get off while we're not looking?' said Damian, looking a little edgy.

Todd broke out laughing. 'They must be going swimming, because nobody gets off till we hit land.'

'Oh yeah,' mumbled Damian, becoming embarrassed, his cheeks reddening.

By the time Todd had taken a number of photographs and had switched places with some of the others they had completed half the trip.

'It doesn't look like a prison. It's more like a holiday camp,' remarked Luke as he shielded his eyes to look at the rocky island with its shabby buildings.

'Are people still locked up there?' asked Sticky.

Todd shook his head. 'No, they haven't had any prisoners here in over thirty years. Only tourists visit these days.'

'Maybe they'll lock up these guys,' said Barbara hopefully.

The children watched with interest as the ferry docked at the lonely Alcatraz jetty. Above them towered the infamous prison's walls. The passengers began streaming onto the pier. The children waited until they saw the two men making their way ashore and then Todd tapped Luke on the shoulder, 'Let's go now. It looks safe. They're well clear.'

The children quickly followed Todd down the steps and across the ramp. The new arrivals were gathering in a semi-circle around a park ranger who was standing on a box.

'Welcome to Alcatraz,' said the ranger by way of a greeting. He was a witty guy and within minutes had the crowd amused and relaxed. He gave a potted history of 'The Rock' as he called it. He explained how it opened in 1859 as an army fort to guard the bay. In 1907 it became a military base and from 1934–63 it served as a maximum-security penitentiary. He told them about several attempted escapes from The Rock.

The ranger then asked the crowd if there were any people from England, Germany, Japan and Australia. People from each country indicated by putting up their hands and shouting out. Then he asked if there was anybody from Ireland.

Simultaneously Luke, Barbara, Damian and Sticky shouted out, 'We are.'

'How's the Blarney Stone?' asked the ranger. 'Have you kissed it recently?'

Todd was cross. 'Keep it down. Don't draw attention to us. We don't want them to know we're following them.'

Luke nodded. 'Okay Todd, sorry. We'll keep it quiet. You heard him, guys.'

The children kept an eye on the two crooks who were hovering on the edge of the crowd. 'What'll we do now?' Luke whispered to Todd.

'I'm not sure. I suppose, keep following them and see

71

what they do next,' he said into Luke's ear. 'They hardly came out here for the scenery.'

'Any questions before we start the tour?' asked the ranger.

'Did anyone ever escape from The Rock?' enquired an elderly man.

The ranger's white teeth flashed a smile. 'Never. Three prisoners disappeared but it's believed that they were drowned. So don't chance it.'

Meanwhile back in San Francisco Mrs Carroll was nervously pacing up and down outside the main entrance to Macys store. Walking to the edge of the street she looked to the right, then the left and then walked back to the entrance.

Within minutes an anxious looking Gordon hurried back to her. By his tense expression she knew he had not found the children.

'No sign of them?' she sighed, already knowing the answer.

He shook his head slowly. 'I've covered two blocks in each direction. I don't know where they could have gone. There are so many stores and coffee shops.'

She frowned. 'This is the spot we arranged to meet them, isn't it?'

'Definitely, exactly here,' he replied with a glum expression. 'Outside Macys. This is the spot.'

Her eyes filled up and she bit her lower lip. 'Where could they be? My lot don't know anywhere round here. They'd be lost if they turned around the corner.'

Gordon was thoughtful. 'Well Todd knows the city like the back of his hand. He shouldn't get lost. I wonder . . . '

'What is it?' she asked urgently.

'That toyshop that Todd likes. I wonder could they be back in there. Maybe we should check it out?'

Immediately Mrs Carroll headed off towards the shop. 'It's hardly likely after two hours but it's worth a try.'

They returned to F.A.O. Swartz and searched every area of the shop without any sign of the children. Gordon spoke to one of the attendants, 'Did you notice five kids all dressed the same in here recently?'

'Oh yeah, earlier to day. They were all over the shop, but not recently,' she explained.

Gordon thanked her and returned with Mrs Carroll to the entrance of Macys. Both of them were growing more frantic by the minute. There was an awkward silence between them.

'What should we do?' asked Mrs Carroll in a hopeless tone.

Gordon gave a deep sigh. 'I don't know. When this is discovered my job is on the line.'

Mrs Carroll turned on him angrily. 'My children are missing in a strange city and all you're worried about is your job. You've got some neck.'

Gordon held up the palms of his two hands towards her. 'I'm sorry. I didn't mean it like that. I just meant I've been Todd's minder for over five years and nothing has ever gone wrong before.'

Luke's mother spoke in a loud voice and waved her finger in Gordon's face. 'Are you blaming my children for losing him?'

'I'm not blaming anyone for anything. I don't know where they are. All I know is that this never happened to Todd before. They could be in a record store, coffee shop

73

. . . anywhere,' he said with frustration.

Their raised voices were beginning to attract the attention of passers-by. Some people slowed down and glared at them. Mrs Carroll blushed and stopped talking as she noticed the scene they were creating. She reached out and touched Gordon's arm, 'I'm sorry Gordon. It's not you're fault. You're as worried as I am.'

He forced a smile. 'I should be the one to apologise. I shouldn't have let them go on their own. I'm totally to blame. I get paid for looking out for Todd . . . and his friends.'

She nodded in response. 'Knowing my pair, five minutes is more like an hour. They don't know the meaning of time. They'll probably turn up sick with sweets and ice cream.'

'I hope you're right. It's just that there have been some fans who think they own Todd. He needs to be protected from them,' Gordon explained in a serious voice.

Mrs Carroll's mouth opened wide and she slowly mouthed the words. 'You mean . . . like kidnap?'

'Well . . . I wouldn't go that far but they'd like a lock of his hair or some of his clothing,' said Gordon, his eyes darting from side to side.

Mrs Carroll's mouth had gone dry with a growing fear. 'Maybe we'd better contact the police then.'

Gordon took his cell phone from a clip on his belt. 'Before I cause a panic I'll do some checking out,' he said as he dialled a number.

'Who are you calling?' she asked.

'It's Todd's cell phone, but I don't think he brought it with him,' he said as he held the phone to his ear. He listened for a few seconds and said, 'Just as I expected.

No go.'

'Could we ring the house? Maybe they went back there,' she suggested.

'And panic his parents if they're not there,' he replied. 'We'll have to think this one out.'

'Oh yes,' she muttered. 'But maybe . . . say I rang and pretended to be Luke's aunt. That might work.'

'Smart thinking,' said Gordon and quickly dialled the number. He handed the cell phone to her.

Her hands were perspiring as she held it to her ear and swallowed hard. She waited. 'Oh hello . . . this is Luke's auntie . . . I wonder is he there at the moment . . . oh, yes . . . I see . . . thank you. I'll call again.' Looking depressed she handed the phone back to Gordon. 'What now?'

Gordon was as confused and upset as Mrs Carroll. 'We can't start an unnecessary panic. You know what kids are like. They could walk around the corner in ten minutes.'

She was forced to agree. 'You're probably right. But they could be in trouble and we're wasting valuable time. Still, it's broad daylight . . . Oh I just don't know the right thing to do.'

'Tell you what . . . we'll wait another thirty minutes. If they haven't shown by then we'll have to notify Todd's parents. After that, if Glen and Harriet agree, we'll ring the cops and start the search,' said Gordon as he consulted his watch.

Mrs Carroll was too stressed to reply and simply nodded. They again began scanning the face of every child that passed.

8
THE JEWELS

Back on Alcatraz the children were unaware of the anxiety their disappearance was causing. From a safe distance they continued to shadow the two crooks. They followed them into the visitor centre where the two men browsed through the bookshop and museum exhibits without much real interest in either. The children were really baffled as the two men sat down in the darkened theatre to watch the audio-visual of the history of Alcatraz. The children sat at the rear and whispered amongst themselves.

'I don't get it. There's something fishy going on here,' said Luke in a soft voice.

'What do you mean?' asked Sticky, sitting beside him.

They all put their heads closer as Luke explained. 'They're just hanging around like the other tourists. Baddies don't do things like that, do they?'

'Beats me. I never saw any crooks before. I wouldn't have a clue,' replied Barbara.

Todd appeared a little disappointed. 'Maybe they're not crooks at all. They might just be weirdos. There's a lot of them hanging around San Francisco. You should see some of them. Even guys dressed as girls.'

'Then what was all the charging around for?' moaned Sticky as he slumped into his seat. 'That wasn't normal, was it? I mean they were in an awful hurry.'

'They might have been trying to catch the boat,' suggested Damian.

'Yeah, probably dead boring after all,' sighed Sticky.

'Could be,' said Barbara. 'But don't ferries go in and out all the time?'

Luke wasn't convinced. 'What about the masks then? Normal people don't wear them.'

Todd thought for a second. 'Maybe it was for a party or something like that.'

'You mean fancy dress?' asked Sticky.

Todd nodded. 'Sure. There are always festivals going on here. The guys are probably harmless.'

Luke wasn't happy with these ideas. 'I hope not. I was looking forward to a good old punch-up and all. And they did clobber that guy, remember? That wasn't normal.'

'What'll we do then?' enquired Todd. 'We've been gone a good bit.'

'Don't know. Say we hang around for a bit more? If nothing happens by then we'll head back,' suggested Luke, as the audio film finished.

Barbara suddenly looked at her watch. 'Oh no, Mam will be up the walls. We were supposed to meet her ages ago.'

Luke jabbed her in the arm with his finger. 'Shush, here they come. Don't let them see us.'

The children lowered their heads as the audience, including the two men, began filing out. At a safe distance the children followed them out of the visitor centre and up the sloping walkway to the cell blocks. There was a menacing feel to the exterior of the two-storey building. Paint peeled from the shabby walls around the barred windows. This was where some of America's most notorious criminals, including Al Capone and Machine Gun Kelly had been imprisoned during the 1940s and '50s. None of the cells had an outside wall or window.

77

As Luke and the others entered the building they were each issued with a set of earphones which gave a running commentary on the history of the prison.

'Hey, this is deadly. I've never been in a prison before,' said a delighted Sticky.

'You'll enjoy it. I made a movie here a couple of years ago. I know every inch of it,' said Todd as he helped the others with the controls of their earphones.

'Can you imagine being locked up for years in a place like this? You'd go stark raving potty,' said Luke as he peered into a small cell with a single bunk and a toilet.

'It would give you the willies,' said Sticky, looking a little uneasy. 'It's eerie – just like Old Ben said.'

Barbara gave a shudder and commented, 'The whole place gives me the creeps. I'd die if I were in here even for a single night. I hope we're not staying for long.'

The children listened to the commentary as they followed the other visitors on the marked route. The two men moved casually with the crowd.

Suddenly Todd tugged at Luke's sleeve. He pointed towards the men. 'They're up to something. Look.'

The two men stood arguing. Luke removed his headpiece to try to hear what they were saying. The fat guy appeared exhausted. 'Hey, will you take the bag again for a bit. People are giving me funny looks.'

'That's you they're looking at, not the bag,' smirked the tall guy.

'I'm serious. It's a ton weight. My arm's broken,' he moaned as he switched the bag from hand to hand.

The tall guy ran his hand through his hair. 'Okay, okay, let me think. Toby won't be here for another couple of hours. We could stash it here for a bit.'

'You mean with the rest of the loot? But only Toby knows where that's hidden. What about the cells up there?' suggested his partner, nodding upwards.

'Okay. Up you go. I'll keep an eye out,' ordered the tall man.

Luke directed the others in behind a wall and put his finger to his lips. They watched as the tall man looked around while his partner stepped over a 'Do Not Enter' sign and climbed the steps to the second floor, continually glancing over his shoulder. Slipping the bag through the bars of the first cell, he quickly returned to join his mate and the pair then made their way out to the exercise yard.

The children remained still, looking from one to the other. They all had puzzled expressions.

'What was that all about?' asked Luke.

Todd shrugged. 'Beats me. They seem to have dumped the bag.'

Luke stepped out into the corridor between the cell blocks. 'Now is the time to find out what's in the bag. Who's on?'

'Are you off your rocker?' cried Barbara. 'I wouldn't go near it. It could be a bomb or anything.'

Todd swiftly clasped his hand over her mouth. 'Keep it down. You don't have to let everyone know.'

'But they could kill us. I want to get out of here. I don't like this at all,' she exclaimed, nervously chewing her thumb.

Luke was thinking fast. 'Knock it off, will you. Okay, I want you guys to check and see if they're still outside while one of you comes back to keep nicks for me and I'll go up for the bag.'

'Are you serious?' asked Damian, his voice holding a warning.

'Deadly serious,' replied Luke as he led them down the corridor. He stopped beside the 'Do Not Enter' sign.

Encouraged by Todd, the others continued along the passageway to a small door. There below them was the high-walled exercise yard, familiar to them from so many films. A water tower threw a shadow across the yard and nearby the two men were sitting smoking on a high step.

'There they are. Pull back. Don't let them see us,' said Todd, drawing back into the doorway.

'What'll we do now?' asked Sticky as he licked his lips.

'Stay put. I'll go to Luke,' ordered Todd, moving back down the corridor. 'Let me know if they look like they're coming back in.'

'Okay,' mumbled Damian, not the least bit happy with the circumstances.

As Todd got within range of Luke he gave him the thumbs-up. Instantly Luke hopped over the sign. He took the steps two at a time. Reaching into the first cell, he snatched the bag and raced back down. With Todd close behind him they continued on down the corridor and sought out a quiet corner. With his heart pounding Luke held up the bag and, ensuring that nobody was watching, quickly jerked it open. He almost fell over with the shock. It was crammed to the brim with jewellery; diamond necklaces and bracelets, watches, earrings and brooches. They both stood staring into the bag.

'There must be a fortune in there,' exclaimed Luke.

'Wow, it's some haul,' said Todd as he touched some of the expensive jewellery.

Perspiration was running down Luke's face and neck with the excitement. 'What do we do now?' he asked.

Todd was puzzled. 'I'm not sure. We can't let them

catch us with it or we'll be finished. On the other hand we can't let them get it back either. Could we hide it somewhere?'

'Brilliant idea. Can you think of anywhere?' asked Luke as he closed the bag.

Todd scratched his chin as he thought. 'I think I know the very place. I remember some bushes around the side of the building. We'll hide it there.'

The two boys walked at a fast pace out of the building. Outside they turned right and quickly continued down a sloping pathway lined with plants and shrubs. Todd stopped, grabbed the bag from Luke and concealed it among the undergrowth. Without exchanging a word they made their way back to the other children.

'Where were you? We were getting really worried.' demanded Barbara.

Damian butted in also. 'It's not fair. Leaving us hanging around for ages. I hate it here. This is no way to spend a holiday.'

'Let me get a word in edgeways and I'll tell you,' said Luke excitedly. 'You'll never guess what was in the bag . . . stacks of jewellery . . . everything you could think of.'

'You're kidding me,' said Sticky in disbelief.

With a beaming face Todd confirmed their find. 'You'd have to see it to believe it. It's full to the brim. Diamonds, jewels – the works. It must be worth thousands. '

'What . . . were you . . . I mean . . . what do we do now?' asked a confused Sticky. '

'Going to the cops would be the best bet,' suggested Todd.'

'Sure that would only take the fun out of it,' said Luke, appearing cocky.

'I'm glad you think it's fun,' said Barbara, heatedly. 'I

certainly don't. I'm really scared. Can we go now?'

Sticky interrupted them. 'Take a look, fellas. They keep checking their watches. I wonder are they waiting for someone or something to arrive?'

Luke peered down at the two men sitting in the sun. 'Must be something like that. Seems a funny place to be hanging around with a bag of jewellery, though. If it were me I'd leg it and be long gone by now.'

'I'd be an awful lot happier if we went back. I'm scared too,' whinged Damian. 'I don't like it here. Just leave the bag and go.'

'Don't be such a baby,' teased Luke giving his friend a light punch in the side. 'We'll show these guys.'

The children settled down for over an hour as the men sunned themselves. Barbara, Sticky and Damian were bored and tired. Luke and Todd were still bubbling with excitement.

'I can't wait to see their faces when they discover that the bag is missing,' said Luke with glee, rubbing his hands. 'It should be classic.'

'Well, you're not going to have long to wait,' said Sticky with urgency in his voice. 'Here they come.'

Damian covered his face with his hands. 'Oh mammy, mammy . . . we're done for.'

'Let's take cover,' snapped Todd.

The children quickly made their way back down the corridor and hid themselves behind walls and doors with good views of the cell where the bag had been stashed.

Within minutes the men strolled casually into the cell block. Giving a quick check that nobody was watching the plump man slipped over the barrier. He made his way up to the cell and reached through the bars. His arm searched around in vain. Next, he jumped up, panic on his face and ran to the two adjoining cells and stared in. Then he danced up and down, waving his arms like a wild man. He charged down the stairs, crashing into the tall man who went sprawling back against the wall.

'It's gone . . . it's gone,' he blurted.

'What the hell's going on?' snarled the other man.

The small man gestured wildly. 'I can't find the bag. It's not where I left it.'

'Let me see.'

The tall crook elbowed him aside. He charged up the stairs and went through the same ritual. He looked into the first cell. Then he crawled along the landing on all fours searching in the half-light. Striking a match he held it against the bars and then flung his arms around in bad tempered gestures. Finally he gave up.

The children watched the scene from their hiding place, half-frightened, half-amused.

The man came down the stairs cursing under his breath. His face was purple with anger, the veins standing out on his forehead. 'Someone's got the bag. Find them and get it,' he ranted.

'And what do we do with them then?'

'Chuck them into the bay for all I care. Let the sharks finish them off. I don't give a damn. Just get the bag before Toby arrives or he'll carve his initials on our guts,' he bellowed as he slammed his clenched fist against the wall.

The men stormed down the corridor towards where Damian was hiding. He was shaking with fright. He was positive they had spotted him. As they got nearer he panicked and ran directly out in front of them. Totally confused, he ran backwards and forwards like a rabbit dazzled by a spotlight. The two men stopped and glared at him. Then putting on a spurt Damian tore past them and belted out through the nearest door.

'That must be the guy who snatched our bag,' shouted the tall man. 'After him. Don't let him get away.'

The crooks took off after Damian.

When the coast was clear the other children gathered in the centre of the cell block.

'Poor Damo,' groaned Barbara.

'He's done for. They'll cut him to ribbons. They're vicious looking,' said Luke, staring towards the door they had passed through.

'They'll kill him if they catch him,' said Sticky, almost in tears. 'Did you see the state of them? They were going spare.'

'And he doesn't even know where the bag is,' sighed Todd.

There was fear in the faces of all the children. They stood about awkwardly, not knowing what to say. Finally Luke said, 'We'll have to find him before they do.'

Todd agreed. 'Luke's right. Let's spread out and search for him.'

'Where'll we begin?' asked Barbara in an anxious voice. 'It's an enormous place. He could be anywhere.'

'We'll just go in different directions and meet up in . . . say the cinema. It's dark there. They won't be able to see us,' suggested Todd as he headed for the main entrance to the cell block.

'That's what we get for following them,' moaned Sticky as he tailed behind. 'It's all your fault, Luke. I told you we shouldn't go but you always know it all.'

'What are you like? Knock it off,' snapped Luke.

'We might never see poor Damo again,' wailed Barbara.

9
TRAPPED

Back in San Francisco Gordon had made the dreaded phone call to Todd's parents. They immediately drove to Union Square and began a heated argument with Todd's minder.

'Your job is to stay with Todd every minute . . . to never let him out of your sight. Don't you understand that?' screamed Mr Harper at Gordon who was attempting to give an explanation.

Mrs Harper was sitting on a park bench almost hysterical. 'My baby . . . my poor baby . . . what's happened to him . . . where is he?' she wailed over and over.

Mrs Carroll put her arms around the woman's shoulder. Despite being distressed herself she did her best to comfort her. 'He'll be all right, Harriet . . . they all will be. They're kids. They probably just wandered off and lost track of time. It happens all the time . . . I know.'

No words of comfort would console Todd's mother. The tears rolled down her cheeks, streaking her mascara and make-up. 'My baby, my baby. He's gone. Will I ever see him again?' she repeated in an uncontrollable whine. 'He's such a wonderful child.'

'Let's just stay calm,' pleaded Mrs Carroll, her eyes bloodshot. 'Did anyone call the police? We've wasted so much time doing nothing.'

'Yeah, yeah, I did that,' replied Mr Harper in an angry

voice. 'They said they'd meet us here. But they're taking their damn time.'

Just then a man in a sports jacket, with a tartan cap pushed back on his head, approached them. 'Okay, everybody. What exactly is going on?' he barked

Mr Harper turned on him sharply. 'Who the hell are you, talking to me like that?'

The man stood face to face with him and flashed his warrant card. 'Lieutenant Rowesome of the SFPD, that's who. Would you put a lid on this pandemonium and would somebody mind explaining what's going on?'

Mr Harper gritted his teeth. 'About time too. Do you know who I am?'

'No,' snarled Rowesome. 'That's why I'm asking. I'm not good at quizzes. Would someone mind answering my questions? I just heard that some kids have gone missing. Big deal. Kids get lost every day. What's new?'

'I'm Glen Harper. My son's Todd Harper. You've heard of him, I suppose?' he said sarcastically.

Rowesomes's brow furrowed. '*The* Todd Harper?'

'The very one. He's gone missing and I want you to pull out all the stops to find him,' demanded Mr Harper.

'My baby's gone. Please find him. He could be hurt or . . . ' bawled Mrs Harper.

Lieutenant Rowesome walked away a few paces from them. 'Look, I can't hear myself think. I just want facts. These hysterics aren't getting us anywhere. Let's have one voice.'

Mr Harper walked over to him and asked, 'What do you want to know?'

'The usual. Where he was last seen. Who he was with. What he was wearing. You know the drill,' he said in a bored voice, rattling off the details.

Mr Harper took a deep breath before answering. 'He was in Macys with Gordon, Mrs Carroll and the Irish kids. They . . .'

'Slow down,' the lieutenant was holding a pad and biro in his nicotine-stained fingers. 'Who's this Mrs Carroll and the Irish kids?'

Todd's father indicated Mrs Carroll standing beside his wife. He went on to explain, 'They're friends Todd met in Ireland last year. They are over on vacation with us and now they've all disappeared together.'

The lieutenant ran a finger over his upper dentures. 'Could the kids have abducted your son?'

Mr Harper shook his head insistently. 'No way, they're all only eleven or twelve. That's not a runner.'

'Okay, you know best. But Todd should be easy to spot. Everybody in the country knows him.'

'True but nobody knows that he's missing,' said Mr Harper, trying to remain calm. 'And besides we dressed all the kids the same to try to camouflage him.'

'We can put a bulletin out on the TV and radio stations asking for information. Were there any phone calls?' enquired the detective.

'How do you mean?'

The detective lowered his voice. 'Making a demand.'

Todd's father exploded. 'You mean a ransom?'

At the mention of this word the two women began crying.

The lieutenant pulled the cap down over his eyes as he moved away. 'I can't handle this. I get enough at home.'

Mr Harper called after him in a startled voice, 'You can't just walk away. What do you intend doing?'

Rowesome spoke over his shoulder. 'Putting a tap on your phone and then giving a description of Todd and the other kids to all precincts – if you tell me exactly what this 'camouflage' they're wearing looks like.'

'Okay, okay, but just find him – them – please,' said Mr Harper in an emotional voice.

On Alcatraz there followed a cat and mouse game between the crooks and the children. Todd, Luke, Barbara and Sticky were trying to find Damian before the crooks discovered his hiding place. Having agreed to regroup in twenty minutes, they each went in a different direction. Todd retraced his steps through the cell block. Barbara went out to the exercise yard. Luke covered the far side of the island. Sticky headed down to the landing jetty. As he approached the area he stopped dead. There ahead of him was the short fat crook, leaning against a wall. He was checking out every person that passed by to board the return ferry to the mainland. Immediately Sticky did an about turn and sprinted back up the hill. He sat shaking on a ledge.

As Luke scouted along an isolated, narrow path above the seashore he noticed a man below at the water's edge. Cautiously he peeked through two bushes. He quickly identified him as the tall man that they had been following. The man appeared to be signalling out to sea. Luke glanced in the same direction and spotted a speedboat heading towards Alcatraz. Huddling up behind the bush he waited to see what would happen next.

'Barbara, Barbara,' called a gentle voice.

Barbara stopped and listened attentively. The voice

seemed to come from a storeroom a few yards away. As she looked, the door opened a crack.

'Barbara, over here,' came the whisper. 'It's me . . . Damian.'

She rushed to the door and swung it open. 'Damian, are you all right? We were so worried.'

Damian's eyes were red from sobbing. 'I want to go home . . . I'm really scared . . . please Barbara . . . '

She didn't know what to say. She was just as frightened and muddled. 'Just wait here and I'll get the others. Don't move. Do you hear me? Stay put.'

Damian swallowed hard. He kept nodding like a toy dog, too scared to speak or move. Barbara dashed away.

Meanwhile Luke watched as the approaching speedboat slowed and moored to a rock at the water's edge. A man dressed in navy and wearing captain's cap stepped ashore.

'Everything in order?' he asked the tall crook abruptly.

The crook began to explain their predicament. 'I'm afraid there's been a hitch, boss.'

'Hitch?' his boss repeated. 'What do you mean, hitch?'

The crook gestured as he spoke. 'The snatch itself went fine. We got out here, hid the bag in one of the cells and waited, but when we went back it had vanished.'

The boss hit him hard across the face. 'Vanished . . . vanished . . . what do you mean? Vanished into thin air? Speak to me, Slater,' he demanded.

The tall crook was jittery as he told his boss the sequence of events and concluded with, 'and when we returned to the cell the bag wasn't there. We saw this kid running off. He must have found it. I don't know.'

'Where did he go?' his boss roared. 'Did he vanish too?

Does everything vanish out here?'

'I'm not really sure, boss. We've been combing the island for him ever since. We haven't let up. Brad's down at the dock checking the ferries. The kid hasn't got a chance, boss. We'll get him. We sure will,' he said determinedly.

The boss snarled, 'You bet your ass. You don't leave the island until the jewellery and that kid turn up. You'll grow old here if you don't. I want every stone turned over.'

'Don't worry, boss. We'll get him,' said the crook, turning to climb up the bank. 'We never let you down.'

'I'm going to dig up the rest of the loot,' said the boss. 'It's getting too hot. The fuzz are sniffing around. I want it all out of here today.'

In a stooped position Luke began to move away slowly and then broke into a run. He continued as fast as he could until he connected up with Todd, Barbara and Sticky. They all began talking at once.

'Where have you been?' sighed Todd.

'Can we get out of here?' pleaded Sticky.

'I found poor Damian. He's in an awful state. He's shaking like a leaf, scared of his life to come out,' sobbed Barbara.

'Good, now listen up everybody. This is important,' cried Luke raising his voice above the others. 'We're in serious trouble. The boss man has arrived and he's really mad. You should see the state of him. He wants the bag and Damo. No messing. He means business . . . big time.'

Barbara bit into her bottom lip trying to hold back the tears. 'Can we not try to get away?'

'Not a chance. The short guy is watching the ferries leaving,' said Sticky. 'They'll nab us for sure if we head down there. We're done for.'

'Okay Barbara, where is Damian?' enquired Todd.

'Come on, follow me. I'll show you,' said Barbara, turning to lead them to Damian's hiding place. Moving cautiously, they were soon gathered outside the storeroom. Barbara tapped lightly on the door. 'Damian, it's me. Open up.' The door inched open. Damian peeped out.

'Ha . . . have they gone yet?' he asked in a broken voice. 'Is . . . is it safe to come out?'

'No, they're searching everywhere. You can't stay here. They'll find you, that's for sure,' said Todd. He wiped perspiration off his brow with the back of his hand.

Luke rubbed his cheek trying to come up with an idea. 'I have it. I saw an old broken-down building at the far end of the island. They'd never think of looking for you there.'

Damian was too scared to move. 'Are you sure it will be safe?'

Luke shrugged. 'Better than here anyway.'

'Let's go then,' instructed Todd, as he opened the door wider.

Frozen with fear, it was a few minutes before Damian could be enticed out. Then all bunched together, the children began to run to an isolated section of the island where no tourists ever visited. Suddenly Sticky tripped and fell sideways. He stumbled over a steep incline and rolled down the bank.

'Help,' he roared out.

Immediately the other children stopped dead in their tracks.

'Hang on. Try and not go into the water,' screamed Luke.

Before Luke had finished speaking Sticky had lost his balance and slid into the sea.

'He'll drown. He can't swim,' screeched Barbara.

'Come on. Quick. We'll have to get him out,' instructed Todd urgently, as he began climbing down the bank.

Luke and Barbara followed quickly behind him. Damian stood in a state of shock, staring down at them. 'But there's sharks in there. You can't. You could be eaten.'

The children picked out hand and foot grips as they eased down towards the water. Sticky was flapping his arms around wildly calling out for help. Then he appeared to be sucked down and disappeared under the waves.

'Oh God, I think he's drowned,' cried Damian in despair.

Seconds later Sticky's head bobbed back above the water like a cork. He was struggling and splashing about frantically.

Todd stretched out to reach Sticky's hand. He was nearly there. 'Just a little more. I need your help, Luke,' he called out with urgency in his voice. Sticky's movements were becoming weaker as the waves engulfed him.

Luke reached Todd and held him around the waist. 'I'll hold you. Go on. Stretch out.'

Todd made another desperate attempt to reach Sticky, stretching his arm out as far as it would go. Just as Sticky was about to go under for the third time, Todd made contact and gripped his wrist. 'I have him . . . I have him . . . pull me in,' he yelled.

'Barbara, quick, grab my belt. I can't hang on,' Luke shouted. She immediately grabbed her brother's belt.

'Pull! Pull me back . . . quick . . . I won't be able to hold on for much longer,' roared Todd as Luke and Barbara formed a human chain.

They pulled with all their might and hauled Sticky out

of the water. He lay on the ground limp and white-faced.

'Is he okay?' Damian called down.

'I hope so, no thanks to you, though,' snapped Luke.

'What now?' asked Barbara.

'Give him the kiss of life, I suppose,' said Todd.

Luke pulled a face. 'You must be joking.'

Todd knelt beside Sticky and turned him onto his back. He tilted Sticky's head a little and began going through the life-saving motions. He repeated it a number of times. Finally Sticky coughed and threw up. He moaned and put his hands over his face. 'Ooh . . . I thought I was a goner. It was horrible.'

'Only for Todd you would have been washed away. You went under twice. You scared the sugar out of us,' said Luke, taking deep breaths.

'Listen, we'd better not hang around here or they'll see us,' said Barbara and she began clambering back up the bank to Damian. Luke and Todd assisted Sticky to his feet. and they followed Barbara.

Back on the mainland the television and radio news bulletins carried reports of the diappearance of Todd and the Irish children. They stated that they were last seen in the Union Square area of the city. They gave a description of the children and what they were wearing. A contact number was given at Lieutenant Rowesome's office.

One person relaxing in a pizza restaurant in the Italian Quarter was particularly interested in the television news. The cab driver remembered picking up a bunch of kids who wanted him to follow a cable car. Lowering his paper, he quickly jotted down the contact number. He went outside to his cab and rang from there and was put through to the lieutenant straight away.

'Are you sure it was them?' asked the detective.

'Sounds like them. I even said it to one of the kids that he was Todd Harper's look-a-like. The kid just laughed and said he was Irish. They all had the same gear on. Looked like a football team. I'd swear it was them,' insisted the cab driver.

Rowesome was growing more convinced by these additional details. 'Where did you drop them?'

The cab driver chewed on the remains of his pizza. 'That's where it gets peculiar – weird like. He said something about catching up with his mother but when I dropped them off they ran after these two guys towards Fisherman's Wharf. I don't get it. Still can't figure it out.'

'Tell me about it! They're kids. They never make sense to me and I've got three of my own. But thanks for your help and if you think of anything else, get back to me,' said the detective.

The cab driver was chuffed at having done his civic duty. 'Sure thing. Hope those kids are safe.'

The lieutenant hung up and straight away and made another call. 'I want every available man posted to the Fisherman's Wharf area with photos of Harper. Ask everyone and anyone if they've seen them,' he ordered.

His next call was to Todd's house. Mr Harper immediately answered the phone.

'Good news. There's been a positive ID of the kids leaving a cab near Fisherman's Wharf. Any idea what they might be doing down there?' asked the detective.

Mr Harper was so muddled with anxiety that he wasn't able to think straight. 'Let me think . . . it could be anything . . . the sea lions . . . the boats . . . anything. Todd loves that area.'

'We're going to comb the place. It won't be long till we find them. By the way, do they know anyone down there?' enquired Rowesome.

Mr Harper didn't like this question. 'Why do you ask?'

'I don't want to alarm you but the cabby said they seemed to be chasing two guys,' he said.

'What! What's that all about?' asked Mr Harper, anxiety again creeping into his voice.

'Beats me,' grunted the lieutenant. 'I have to go. Too much to do. I'll keep you posted.' He hung up and headed out of his office.

Within half an hour forty police had been assigned to check out the area around Fisherman's Wharf. They were each issued with a photograph of Todd and descriptions of the other children and were instructed to speak to vendors, musicians, stallholders, coffee shop staff and tourists.

10
TERROR

At the pier head on Alcatraz an announcement was made over the tannoy system: 'The last ferry for San Francisco leaves the island in fifteen minutes.'

'We're sure to get him now. He'll have to come out,' Brad stated confidently as he paced up and down the jetty.

Toby didn't seem so certain. 'Are you sure he hasn't slipped out already?' he grunted.

The stocky man's face twitched with annoyance. 'I'm nearly a hundred per cent sure, boss. I saw everyone going past, unless he's made himself invisible.'

'Nearly?' repeated Toby with venom in his voice. 'Nearly isn't good enough for me. If we don't get that bag you won't be heard of again. Your neck's on the block.'

'There's no need for that. It wasn't my fault. Slater and I followed your instructions to the letter,' Brad declared as the last of the tourists filed onto the ferry.

Toby pointed a bony finger. 'Just find him. Nobody mucks me around. You don't eat, sleep, sit down . . . anything . . . until the bag and the kid are both found.'

Luke watched from above the pier. He'd volunteered to scout around but was growing more despondent with every passing minute. Their only route of escape had now been cut off. He decided that he'd better return to the others and bring them up to date with the bad news. He ran as fast as he could. He was almost breathless when he reached the derelict building where the others were hiding.

'The last ferry's about to leave. What are we going to do? If we miss it we're stuck here till tomorrow,' said Luke, as he sat panting on a pile of blocks.

Sticky seemed slightly relieved. 'But the bad guys will have to go then, won't they?'

Luke didn't appear happy. He shook his head slowly. 'No way. They have a speedboat of their own, remember. If we show our noses we're goners.'

'Then we're stuck here!' yelled Damian.

'Trapped on Alcatraz, I don't believe it,' added Sticky.

Todd gestured to keep down the noise. 'Shush it, guys. Do you want someone to hear us?'

'Does that mean we're going to have to stay here all night?' enquired Barbara with a tremor in her voice.

Luke hung his head, his breathing back to normal. 'I don't want to even think about it.'

'Will nobody help us?' cried Sticky, holding the top of his head with his two hands.

'What about Gordon and your mam, Luke? They're probably out searching for us but not in a million years would they think of looking here,' sobbed Damian.

Todd nodded with a grim face. 'If only there was some way of contacting my home. I normally carry a cell phone with me . . . but not today. Damn it.'

Luke looked thoughtful for a while and then said,' I think we'll just have to bed down here for the night, and hopefully we can make a run for it in the morning. They'll probably be long gone by then.'

Barbara's expression was one of fear. 'Stay here all night . . . are you out of your mind? It'll be pitch black and I hate the dark and I'm starving . . . and . . . and there could be all sorts of creepy crawlies around. Are you mad?'

'And Old Ben said it was haunted and that Al Capone and the others wandered around at night,' said Sticky with a shiver.

'Don't make it any worse. If we stay together we should be okay. I'm sure my dad has every cop in San Francisco searching for us,' said Todd, making an effort to calm them.

'I need something to eat too,' whined Sticky. 'I'm starving.'

'You would be,' muttered Damian, growing impatient with his complaining. 'You'll be on your death bed and you'll still be looking for food. There's nothing to eat here, so belt up yapping about it. You're making us all hungry.'

Sitting down among the debris the children tried to make themselves as comfortable as possible. Sticky was still soaking wet. As darkness descended on their island prison the children became colder and more scared. They tried to sleep but realised there was little chance of that happening. Gradually they got tired talking and dozed on and off.

Twilight was settling over Fisherman's Wharf. A cop approached the hatch at the Blue and Gold Fleet booking office. He flashed a photograph of Todd in front of the attendant. 'Have you seem this kid?' he asked in a dreary voice for the umpteenth time.

'Hey, isn't that Todd Harper, the movie star?' declared the girl in a loud voice.

The cop nodded. 'Sure is. Have you seen him around here today?'

'Can't say I have,' she replied, '. . . but hey . . . '

The cop became alert. 'What is it?'

'Yeah . . . yeah . . . the guy on the earlier shift said that some famous kid went out to Alcatraz today. Didn't mention a name though. Was it him?' she enquired.

'I hope so. He's gone missing. Where's your colleague?' said the cop, taking his walkie-talkie out of its holder.

The attendant scratched her chin. 'Eh . . . he went off duty about two hours ago. He's got no phone but I can give you his address.'

'Great. Just jot it down. I want to call the precinct,' said the cop with growing confidence.

As night closed in on Alcatraz, the only sign of life was the beam from the lighthouse. The children were jittery. They jumped at the slightest sound. Suddenly there was a strange trembling sensation. They were startled.

Damian cried out, 'Oh my God . . . what was that?'

'I think it was a tremor,' replied an exhausted Todd.

'From . . . from an earthquake?' said Barbara, forcing out the words.

Luke half stood. 'Will we be killed?'

Todd shrugged but sounded frightened. 'There might be an after-shock or another quake or maybe nothing.'

Sticky quickly blessed himself. 'Oh please God there won't be any more.'

'I wonder is the speedboat gone?' asked Todd, as he thought out loud.

Luke lifted his head at this enquiry. 'Maybe it is. Do you want me to check it out?'

'But it's pitch black. You'll break your neck,' mumbled Sticky. 'You won't be able to see your hand.'

Luke, although frightened, tried to sound defiant. 'I'm

99

not afraid of the dark. Anyone want to tag along?'

There was silence for a while. Then Todd volunteered, 'Hang on. I'll go with you.'

'Are you both stark raving mad? You'll only hurt yourselves or else they'll catch you. Don't go out there,' whispered Barbara in a nervous voice.

'Anything's better than just hanging around doing nothing. If the speedboat's still there maybe we can get away in it,' said Luke standing and stretching his legs.

Barbara glared at him. 'What are you on about? You can't drive a boat, you eejit. You'll kill yourself.'

'It's simple, so it is,' he replied. 'Just like driving a car.'

His sister came back fast. 'Come off it. You don't know how to drive a car either . . . or anything else.'

'I do so. I'm always watching Mam and Dad doing it. Bet you anything I can,' he said confidently.

Todd tugged at his sleeve. 'We're wasting time, Luke. Let's go.'

Sticky forced back the door for them. Todd squeezed through the opening into the pitch blackness, followed by Luke. Neither of them let on to the other that they didn't like the idea of walking down the slope in the dead of night. 'I think I know the way,' said Luke as he cautiously made his way in the dark. 'It's over there by the cliffs somewhere.'

They continued on in silence, step by step, making slow progress.

Suddenly Luke crashed into something dark. 'What the . . .' he shrieked.

'I knew you'd be back,' snarled Toby as he grabbed Luke tightly by the shoulders.

Todd froze with fear. 'Who is it . . . what are . . . ?'

'Run . . . run . . . run . . . Todd,' screamed Luke. 'Don't let them get you. Run!' Todd turned and, half-running, half-stumbling, he fled back into the darkness.

'Don't just stand there. Get him, you fools,' yelled Toby at his two henchmen.

Unable to see anything, Brad and Slater collided with each other and fell in a heap to the ground. They cursed and grumbled at each other as they stood up.

'Forget it,' snarled Toby as he turned his attention to Luke. 'We have this one. He'll tell us all we want to know. Where's the bag?'

'Eh . . . I'm not sure,' mumbled Luke, terrified.

Toby shook him vigorously. 'You better be sure because we've got ways of dealing with troublesome kids. How would you cope without your tongue for example?'

Luke tried to shake himself free but the man's grip was too tight. 'Oh no, no . . . please,' cried Luke. 'I mean it's dark and I can't see anything. I think I know where the bag is . . . I'm not sure . . . but the other kids definitely do.'

'Do you want me to sort him out?' asked Brad. 'See how he likes being without his fingernails.'

'No. Just tie him up for now,' instructed Toby. 'We'll wait till the morning.'

They escorted Luke to the outside wall of the exercise yard. They tied his hands and feet and left him lying by the wall. Although Luke was really scared he began thinking of some way to escape. He realised that these guys meant business. They wouldn't think twice about sticking a knife between his ribs or a bullet in his head. He had to get away.

'Huh, time is valuable to me. When it gets bright you pair get the other kids. I'll work on this guy. See if his memory comes back,' grunted Toby.

By the time Todd made his way back to the derelict house he was tired and scared. He burst in with such a racket that he terrified the others. His legs were trembling so much that he had to lean against the wall to recover.

'They've got Luke . . . they've got Luke . . . ' he screamed over and over.

Barbara began sobbing, 'Is . . . is . . . he . . . ?'

'I don't know! He told me to run and that's what I did,' he explained in a broken voice.

'Poor old Luke . . . and it was me they were after,' sniffled Damian. 'What can we do?'

'I don't know. It's pitch black out there. You can't see your hand. We'll have to wait till the morning or we'll fall into the bay,' sighed Todd.

'I hope they won't hurt him. He gets on my wick at times but he isn't a bad brother,' sniffed Barbara. '

'Maybe the cops will find us by then,' said Sticky, adding an air of encouragement.

The children huddled together. They settled down on the floor and tried to make themselves comfortable.

11
THE ROUNDUP

Barbara woke with a start, aware of a curious noise which grew louder. 'Listen,' she called to the others. 'Can you hear that sound?'

'What is it?' asked Sticky.

'It's weird. I can't make it out,' she answered.

The children remained dead quiet and listened attentively.

Todd jumped to his feet and announced, 'It's a chopper. I know that sound. I think they've come for us.'

Damian wasn't so sure. 'Be careful, Todd. It might be those crooks again.'

'There's only one way to find out,' said Todd, as he pulled open the door. A shaft of sunlight brightened the inside of the building.

In a distressed, weary voice Damian said, 'It's daylight. The crooks'll see us for sure – we're mincemeat now.'

'Yes, it's a chopper but it's the cops. We're okay, guys . . . we're okay,' cried Todd excitedly.

The children jumped to their feet and rushed outside. They all shouted and waved frantically as the police helicopter flew in low over the island.

'We're saved, we're saved!' cheered Barbara as she danced about.

There was a look of disbelief on Damian's face as he pointed behind her. 'Oh no we're not. We're trapped.' The children all spun round to see the two crooks charging up the hill towards them.

'Let's scarper,' cried Sticky as he began to run.

Todd stood his ground. 'No, we won't run. Let's throw some of these bricks at them. There's more of us than them. ' He swiftly bent to pick up a brick from the mound lying around their feet. He threw it but it fell short. The other children began flinging bricks at the two men. Damian hit the short man on the arm. Sticky scored a direct hit on the forehead of the tall man, who clutched his head and doubled over. An array of bricks and stones, fired in quick succession, rained down on the men, hitting them on the arms, chests, legs and heads.

'Stop . . . you'll kill us,' cried Brad holding up his hands.

The children slowly approached them, holding a brick in each hand as the helicopter hovered overhead. 'This is the SFPD. Stand still. Put your hands in the air and don't move,' called Lieutenant Rowsome through a megaphone. The crooks stood with their bloodstained hands in the air.

The helicopter landed nearby and armed police, wearing bullet-proof vests, jumped to the ground. Guns at the ready, they ran up behind the two men. The crooks were roughly bundled onto the ground and quickly handcuffed.

A burly sergeant approached the children and asked, 'Are you kids okay?'

Todd spoke first. 'We're fine. Nobody's hurt.'

Barbara interjected, 'But they've got my brother, Luke.'

The sergeant patted her on the shoulder, 'Don't worry about him, honey. We'll soon have him back safe and sound.' He then escorted the children to the helicopter to have them flown back to the city.

On the other side of the island Toby still held Luke captive. His fingers dug into the boy's shoulders as he shook him. 'Has your memory come back yet, kid? Do you remember where the bag is?'

Luke realised that he had no choice. He decided to show the man where it was concealed. The police were nearby – he was sure he'd heard the buzz of a helicopter. If he could stall long enough he would soon be rescued.

'Eh . . . it's down here . . . in the bushes.'

'That's what I like to hear,' said Toby as he pushed Luke on at a faster pace.

'If I show you will you let me go?' Luke asked brazenly.

Before Toby had time to reply Luke spotted another police helicopter and two police motor launches approaching Alcatraz from the mainland. Although scared, he felt excited by the activity – this was his wildest dream come true.

Toby's fury increased. 'Don't worry, they won't get me that easily,' he said angrily.

'There's the bag,' said Luke nodding towards the bushes. 'Can you untie my arms, they hurt?'

Toby reached in and grabbed the bag. 'No chance. Now let's show the cops how fast we can move.'

'Please, can I go now?' pleaded Luke, feeling uneasy with the man's threatening tone.

Toby sneered at him. 'Why should I let you go? Aren't you enjoying yourself? You'll make a fine shield.'

He grabbed Luke tightly by the arm and charged along the path. They slid down the sandy bank to where the speedboat was tied to some undergrowth. Toby steadied the boat with his foot, roughly flung Luke into it and leaped in behind him. There were several other bags and briefcases already on the floor. The engine started with a roar and the boat surged away from the island.

'Hope you like speed,' he said with a mad laugh.

Luke was so low down in the boat that he could not see what was happening. Toby kept him clamped to the floor with his foot pressed against his back. Luke wriggled his wrists and arms to try and free them from the rope.

As the speedboat streaked across the water, the police motor launches and helicopter changed course and gave chase. The speedboat skimmed the waves as it headed for the waterfront and Luke was buffeted from side to side like a cork. The distance between the speedboat and motor launches lengthened but the helicopter still hovered above them. A voice addressed them: 'This is the SFPD. Cut your engine and prepare to be boarded.'

Toby shook his fist in the air as a gesture of contempt, turned sharply and headed the boat directly towards Pier 43. There was a loud grating sound as the speedboat collided with the wooden pier. Toby grabbed Luke with one hand and picked up the bags with the other. He hauled Luke out of the boat and up the steps. Luke was really scared and knew that he had better cooperate with Toby if he wanted to survive.

As Toby pushed and dragged Luke down the pier towards the road some of the bags began dropping from his grasp. Suddenly Luke realised that Toby couldn't escape. It was only a matter of time before the cops nailed him.

A number of cops from the motor launches were running down the pier behind them and the police helicopter was monitoring their every move from overhead.

The homeless old man Luke and Todd had bumped into the previous day was roused from his shelter on the footpath. He watched as Toby and Luke rushed by. Then he noticed a small bag beside his trolley. He picked it up and opened it – it was full of ten and twenty dollar bills! The shock was so great that he had to lean against the wall to steady himself. He scratched his weather-beaten face before taking a second peep inside the bag. It was for real. There were thousands of dollars inside the bag. Quickly he closed it up and concealed it under the blanket in the trolley and began shuffling along the footpath.

Crossing the road, Toby reached into his belt and drew out a revolver. He stopped and held the gun to the windscreen of the first car that approached them.

'Out . . . out . . . out,' he screamed at the driver.

All the colour drained from the driver's face and without hesitation he scrambled from his seat. Toby shoved Luke headfirst across into the passenger's seat and bundled the bags in on top of him. He then moved quickly behind the controls. As the car screeched away, a fleet of patrol cars, lights flashing, sirens blaring, sped after them.

Luke felt sore and uncomfortable trussed up like a turkey. He made a last determined effort to free himself and succeeded in partially freeing one of his hands. Toby was too busy avoiding the roadblocks to notice Luke's actions. He was driving like a madman. The car screeched around corners and scraped against parked cars. Luke was positive they were going to be killed if he did not do something fast.

Stretching across, he grabbed Toby tightly by the leg, and then, opening his mouth wide, sank his teeth into his thigh. Toby gave an ear-piercing yell and stooped down to hold his leg. The car went out of control, the steering wheel spinning with such force that it was wrenched from Toby's hands. The car careered across the road and hit a wall. The windscreen shattered in on top of them.

Dazed and shaken, Luke blinked and saw drops of blood on his arm. But it was Toby's blood – he was slumped over the steering wheel, his head gashed, blood trickling from the wound over his eye.

With guns drawn cops ran from their patrol cars and surrounded the car. 'Out you get, kid,' said one of the cops as he assisted Luke from the floor. 'Nice and easy.'

'Is he dead?' enquired Luke in a soft voice.

'Don't mind him. He'll be sorted out. You're the important one,' smiled the police officer as he led Luke towards a waiting ambulance.

Luke wriggled free from him and said, 'I'm okay, I don't need anything.'

There was considerable activity as more cops arrived and swarmed around the crashed car. Toby was lifted out by two paramedics and placed on a stretcher.

'Luke . . . Luke . . . what was it like?' cried Todd's familiar voice. Luke spun around to spot Todd shouldering himself through the police line. They embraced each other. 'Did he hurt you?' asked Todd. 'Are you okay?'

Luke beamed. 'Great. Never felt better. It was deadly. Being in a boat chase and a car chase and all. It was like a James Bond film. I'd love to do it all again.'

Soon Barbara, Damian and Sticky had gathered around him firing questions. 'I thought you were really a goner,' said Damian in a serious voice. 'Especially when I saw the gun.'

Luke laughed and asked, 'What happened to the other guys? Did the cops get them?'

'Only when we'd finished with them. We pelted them with bricks,' explained Barbara with relish.

'You should have seen the state of them. They were bursted open,' added Sticky.

'Sorry I missed that,' remarked Luke. 'I would have—'

Before he could finish the sentence his mother had run up and wrapped her arms around him and smothered him in kisses. 'Luke, Luke, did they hurt you? I never thought I'd see you again.'

Luke, highly embarrassed, broke away from her. 'Mam, will you give over. You're making a show of me. I'm fine. It's no big deal.'

She bit her lip to prevent herself crying. 'Did he hurt you? You're sure you're not in pain?'

He jumped into the air and waved his arms about. 'Look I'm as good as new. Leave me, Mam I'm grand.'

Then she noticed blood on his arm and some more on his T-shirt. 'My God, look at your arm. It's cut. We'll have to get you to hospital.'

Luke licked his hand and rubbed the blood on his arm away. 'It's not mine. It's from your man in the car. You should see the state of him. He's in bits.'

Mrs Carroll sighed and began to breathe more easily.

They were soon joined by Gordon, Todd's parents and Lieutenant Rowsome. The detective addressed the children in a stern voice. 'Let that be a warning, kids. You put your lives in danger tangling with that gang. Any one of them would have slit your throat without giving it a second thought. Between them they have a list of convictions the length of the bridge. You're lucky you're not being carted away in one of those,' he said, indicating an ambulance.

'I'm sorry. It was all my fault,' said Todd, his cheeks reddening.

Luke shook his head and spoke loudly. 'No, it was mine. I suggested following them. Todd's not to blame.'

The lieutenant smiled. 'Listen kids, you can sort this one out between yourselves. Don't mind what I just said. We're very grateful to you. We've been trying to track this gang for over two years. Little did anyone know that they would use Alcatraz to stash the proceeds of their robberies. We've dug up quite a haul. Thanks a lot but no more heroics, okay?'

Todd nodded shyly. 'We won't. I promise.'

'Hey kids, will you turn this way,' instructed an unfamiliar female voice behind them.

The children turned around to find a television reporter and a camera crew before them.

'I'd like to do an interview with you,' she began as she held the microphone towards Todd. Before he had time to respond she was asking her first question. 'Well Todd, were you scared being trapped on Alcatraz all night?'

Todd smiled,' I was, but it was my buddies from Ireland who were the real heroes. They were fantastic, especially Luke who made the guy in the getaway car crash it.'

'Really?' exclaimed the astonished reporter moving her attention to Luke. 'Tell me Luke, how did you manage it? Was your life in danger?'

Luke came over bashful and replied in his best voice. 'Well, when he held me hostage and I saw the gun I knew I was a goner if I didn't do something.'

'And what happened?' she asked.

'When I managed to free myself from the ropes I bit his leg, you know. Then he sort of went spare and crashed. It was deadly,' he explained in one breath.

The reporter blinked. 'And has this incident put you off coming back to San Francisco?'

'No way. It's mad here. The best. I'd love to stay. Things

like this never happen in Bray,' said Luke with a burst of enthusiasm.

'Thank you very much . . . eh . . .' she began to turn away.

Luke grabbed the microphone and kept speaking. 'Luke Carroll, and this is Sticky and Damo and my sister, Barbara, and everybody knows Todd Harper. We think it's deadly here and we would all love to come back.'

The reporter grew impatient with his rambling and stated bluntly into the camera, 'That is all from Cathy Norton. Now back to the studio.'

Soon other reporters had surrounded the children and were asking them questions about their ordeal. While they were giving the details several photographers were snapping away.

'This is getting better every minute. We'll be on the telly and in the papers and all,' cried Sticky. 'They think we're heroes.'

But Mrs Carroll was in a serious mood. 'It's not good enough, running away like that. Did you know the stress you put Mr and Mrs Harper through? What were you thinking about?'

Luke spoke up. 'We didn't mean to. It was a bit of gas, you know. We saw this jeep —'

Mrs Harper placed her hand on Luke's head. 'They're okay, Andrea. It's all over. We'll leave it for now.'

Mr Harper spoke to the detective. 'Um . . . are you through, Lieutenant Rowesome? Can we go now?'

'By all means. I'll drop around and get a statement later,' grinned the detective. 'And if any of you guys fancy joining the police force give me a shout in eight or ten years' time. That goes for you too, Barbara.'

111

'Are you serious?' asked Luke in an excited voice.

His mother began guiding them away. 'Don't start, Luke. You've had enough excitement for two lifetimes. I don't want you getting any more notions.'

'Thanks for everything, Lieutenant,' said Mrs Harper, shaking him warmly by the hand.

He shrugged. 'Just doing my job, ma'am. Best of luck. Can we give any of you guys a lift home?' he asked as he turned to leave.

'Oh yes please,' volunteered Luke.

His mother shook her head in amusement, 'Trust you, Luke. You never miss an opportunity.'

The lieutenant called to one of the cops. 'Will you run these kids home?'

'Sure thing, Lieutenant,' he replied, opening the rear door of the patrol car. All the children quickly bundled in.

The old homeless man was standing nearby, smiling and observing the activity. He patted the bag of money in his shopping trolley and walked away.

'Enjoying this, kids?' smiled the cop, as they sped along the coast.

'Not half. It's brilliant,' replied a spellbound Luke.

'I've never been in a police car before,' said Sticky, leaning on the back of the seat.

'Any chance you could put on the siren?' asked Todd.

'Sure thing. It's the least we can do for you guys,' laughed the cop as he flicked on the siren and flashing blue light.

A thrill of excitement ran through the children as they raced through the streets and cars pulled in allowing them to pass. The journey was all too short and soon they had reached the Harpers' house. Then it was a hot bath, a change of clothes and a delicious meal for the children. Mrs Carroll insisted that they all go to bed for a rest. Although they lay down, there was no sleeping as they each relived every second of their adventure.

A few hours later they all gathered around the television to watch the tea-time news. A big cheer went up from the children when the car chase was screened and the reporter described the incident on Alcatraz. She stated that the children were 'the heroes of the day'.

'Look at the state of you. You're filthy. Like homeless urchins,' commented Mrs Carroll, laughing at the TV.

Luke gave her a playful punch on the arm. 'Tell you what, Mam, we could get into our good clothes and do it all again tomorrow.'

'You would if you got half a chance,' smiled his mother.

'We must get you a video of that news report to bring home and show your buddies,' said Mr Harper proudly.

'This is brill. It gets better all the time,' said a chuffed Luke.

12
THE PREMIERE

With the excitement of the robbery the purpose of the children's visit to San Francisco had almost been overlooked – the premiere of *Orphans' Retreat*.

First thing the next morning Todd bounced into the boys' room and woke them from a deep sleep.

'Wakey, wakey, guys. This is the big day,' cried Todd as he clapped his hands and drew back the blinds. The sun streamed in through the window.

'What . . . what day?' asked Luke as he opened one eye. 'What are you on about?'

'Will you keep it down. I can't sleep,' mumbled a weary voice from under the blankets in Sticky's bed.

Mischievously Todd tiptoed to the bed and peeled back the covers. Sticky was curled up in a ball.

'You're going to miss it,' laughed Todd.

'Miss what?' asked Damian, sitting upright in his bed.

Todd opened the door and called out, 'Gordon, you can bring them in now.'

Gordon entered the room with a number of suit bags draped over his arm. 'Let's try these for size, guys.'

By now they were all sitting up in their beds rubbing their eyes. Gordon left one bag on each of their beds.

Luke hopped onto the floor and unzipped the bag. 'Hey, what's this? Some sort of monkey suit,' he cried with disbelief.

Sticky held up his suit. 'What are these for? Is it a fancy

dress or something?'

Todd doubled up laughing at their reactions. 'To wear at the film premiere tonight. There's one for everyone.'

Luke flung it onto the bed with distaste. 'No way. I wouldn't be caught dead in something like that. Are you having me on?' he sighed.

'I knew it was too good to last. Are you sure it's not April Fool's Day?' moaned Damian.

Gordon tried to conceal his amusement and announced, 'Okay, I'll gather them up. Nobody's being forced.'

He had picked up two of the suits when Luke spoke again. 'What happens if we don't wear them?'

'You can't go. Even Gordon, my dad and myself will have to wear them. Nobody will be let in without dress suits. It's a gala premiere. All the stars will be there,' explained Todd, used to the procedure at such events.

Luke muttered and punched his pillow. 'I'll never be able to live it down. It's dire. If anybody saw me it would be death.' He hesitated for a while and then said, 'Okay, I'll try it on . . . but only for you, Todd.'

Gordon winked at Todd as he replaced the suits on the beds. Reluctantly the three boys changed into the junior-size dress suits – black pants and jacket, a bow tie, fluffy white shirt and black patent shoes.

'I feel a right prat,' mumbled Sticky.

'Let's show the rest of them. See what they think,' suggested Todd. With red cheeks and embarrassed expressions the three boys trudged along the landing and down the stairs. They felt self-conscious. Todd's parents stood up as they entered the lounge.

'Gee, you guys look cute,' said Mrs Harper.

'Cute,' thought Luke to himself. This was one word

which had never been attributed to him before.

'You all look very smart,' added Mr Harper.

While the boys stood mortified, being admired by the Harpers, the door opened. In walked Barbara and her mother dressed in glamorous evening gowns. Mrs Carroll wore a crimson off-the-shoulder dress. Barbara wore a long turquoise gown. She appeared very grown up.

'Wow, look at these two glamorous ladies,' said Mr Harper admiringly.

Mrs Carroll's cheeks grew pink. 'I've never worn anything so beautiful . . . it's really sensational.'

Mrs Harper smiled warmly. 'I was hoping for the best, Andrea and it fits you perfectly. You do it justice.'

Luke stared at his mother and sister with his mouth wide open. 'I . . . I . . . never saw you like that before,' he stuttered.

'And you look a proper little gent . . . all of you do,' said his mother as she inspected the trio and straightened their bow ties.

'Oh by the way, take a look at these,' said Mrs Harper as she indicated a bundle of newspapers on the table.

Todd lifted up the top paper. He scanned the front page. It read 'Todd Harper and Young Heroes Foil Crooks on Alcatraz'. Immediately beneath the headline there was a photograph of himself and the other children.

'Wow, would you take a squint at that,' exclaimed Luke loudly. 'We're on the front page. It's our picture.'

The other children jostled around him and grabbed the paper. Luke flicked through the other papers in which they also featured on the front pages.

'This is deadly . . . massive . . . the best ever,' screeched Sticky as he closely inspected the photographs.

'Would you look at the state of me. I look like a witch,' said Barbara, seeing herself in one of the papers.

'Well done everybody. I'm proud of you,' said Mrs Carroll with a lump in her throat.

'We're all proud of you, even if it was foolhardy,' agreed Todd's mother. 'Now,' she continued, 'the clothes seem to be a fine fit. You can change out of them now if you like.'

'I can't wait. I feel a right wally,' cried Luke running from the room.

Sticky and Damian quickly followed him back to their bedroom. With great relief they changed into their casual clothes.

'I thought I was going to enjoy the cinema but nobody said anything about being dressed up like a dog's dinner,' moaned Damian.

'Don't remind me about it,' added Sticky.

'Can you imagine turning up at the Royal in Bray in gear like that? They'd lock you up,' sighed Damian.

The remainder of the day was hectic. There were visits to the hairdresser's for everybody. A buffet was laid on for lunchtime with a table laden with goodies – salmon, turkey, ham, salads, an assortment of ice creams and strawberries. The children made gluttons of themselves.

'Make sure that you don't eat too much now. You'll have a lot more to eat before the day is finished,' warned Todd.

'I'll worry about that when the time comes,' said Sticky, licking his fingers.

In late evening they all changed into their formal clothes. A photographer from the film company was assigned to remain with them all night, photographing anything appropriate.

117

At seven o'clock two stretch limos drew up outside the front door.

'We'll let the children travel together in the first one, if that's all right with you?' Todd's father asked Mrs Carroll.

Mrs Carroll, appearing very chic in her new dress and styled hair, smiled in response, 'That's fine with me.'

The Irish children felt very important as they walked out and climbed into the back of the stretch limo.

Barbara felt butterflies in her stomach. 'God, I won't know what to do or say. I'm in bits,' she said nervously.

Todd tapped her lightly on the arm. 'You'll be fine. Everybody will be mad about you. I promise.'

The film premiere was to be held in the Metreon Entertainment Centre. It was located at Fourth and Mission. It consisted of fifteen state-of-the-art movie theatres, 3-D interactive electronic games and a selection of restaurants. Outside the cinema, crash barriers held back hundreds of eager fans waiting to see the stars arrive. A red carpet stretched from the sidewalk to the main entrance. Enormous arc lamps and lasers lit up the night sky and illuminated the occupants as they emerged from each new stretch limo. Television crews interviewed the celebrities as they proceeded up the red carpet. A battery of photographers flashed away at every new arrival.

'Wow, would you take a look at that. It's like the Oscars or Eurovision or something,' said Luke with his face pressed against the window.

Damian nervously fidgeted with his fingers. 'I don't want to go in there. It looks dangerous. You could be crushed.'

'You'll be great, Damo. Just follow me,' grinned Todd with confidence as they pulled up outside the cinema.

'Nothing will happen to you.'

As the limo stopped alongside the barrier, Gordon stepped out and opened the door. Todd sprang out onto the red carpet. A tremendous scream went up from the frantic fans. They chanted, 'We love Todd, we love Todd.'

'My God, would you take a look at that. They're stark raving mad,' said Luke, frozen to his seat. 'They'd tear you apart.'

Todd bent down and called in, 'Come on, guys. It's great. They won't bite you.'

With his nails dug into the clammy palms of his hands Luke stepped out, the others piling out behind him. The fans screamed all the louder. Todd grabbed Luke by the hand and held it above his head in a sign of triumph. They moved slowly up the red carpet, looking from side to side, and all the while the cameras flashed.

'You'd swear we were pop stars,' whispered Damian. 'It's something else.'

'This way, Todd,' shouted a fan.

He looked left and right as fans and photographers called his name.

Finally they reached the lobby of the building where there were hundreds of glamorously dressed people standing about chatting. People crossed over to shake hands with Todd. He introduced Luke and the other children to them.

After a while an announcement was made that everybody should take their seats. The children filed inside and were escorted to their seats mid-way down the cinema.

'This place is massive,' remarked Sticky. 'Yeah, heaps bigger than the Royal,' added Damian.

Gordon appeared beside them. He had a large container

of popcorn and a coke for each of them.

Soon the lights were dimmed. The white suited compere walked to the centre of the stage. 'You're all welcome to the world premiere of *Orphans' Retreat*. It gives me great pleasure to introduce the young star of the film . . . our very own . . . TODD HARPER. Let's have you, Todd.'

There was an enthusiastic round of applause as Todd ran up the aisle and onto the stage.

Luke was bubbling with excitement. 'Isn't this deadly. It's like you see in the films. I wouldn't go up there for any money.'

The compere held the microphone to Todd and asked him, 'Well Todd, this movie is a complete new departure for you. It's your first costume film. How did it feel?'

'Cold, especially as I only wore rags and no shoes,' replied Todd with a grin.

There was a loud ripple of laughter from the audience.

'Indeed. That must have been uncomfortable. And this was your first movie abroad . . . in Ireland. What was that like?' asked the compere.

'Brilliant. That was the best part of the whole thing because I met my new buddies over there. They were in the movie too. I'd like to call them up . . . Luke, Damian, Sticky and Barbara,' cried Todd.

The children were all dumbfounded. They sat looking at each other. Nobody moved.

Todd shouted down at them, 'Come on guys . . . everybody's waiting.'

Mr Harper, sitting behind them, prodded Luke in the back. 'Up you go, Luke . . . go on, all of you. They're waiting.'

Luke swallowed hard. Then warily he stepped into the aisle. The others stood up nervously behind him.

Todd waved frantically and called out, 'We're waiting . . . the movie will be over before you get up.'

In single file and appearing totally mortified Luke and the children marched up to the stage. They kept their eyes focused on the floor.

'So what was it like being in the movie with Todd?' asked the compere.

'Who . . . me?' mumbled Luke.

The compere spoke louder and held the microphone closer to Luke. 'Yeah, did you enjoy working with Todd?'

'Oh yeah, yeah . . . it was deadly,' said Luke in a soft voice.

Todd leaned over and spoke loudly, 'And these are the kids from the big roundup on Alcatraz yesterday. They're the heroes. They caught the crooks.'

At this news there was another enthusiastic round of applause. The compere thanked the children. Blushing, heads down, they returned to their seats. The director and some of the other actors were then introduced.

Then the cinema darkened and the credits rolled for *Orphans' Retreat*. From the opening scene the children were able to identify the Irish locations. When Todd first appeared there was a gasp from the children.

Todd whispered to Luke, 'Watch out. You're coming up soon.'

Luke leaned forward, his hands grasped on his lap, waiting.

Then Luke, Sticky, Damian and all the other orphans appeared, walking barefooted up the mountain track.

'There I am,' exclaimed Damian.

'And me,' added Sticky.

'Would you take a look at the state of my hair. It's dire,'

cried Luke covering his eyes with his hands. The children oohed and aahed as they settled back and enjoyed the film. As the final credits rolled there was a wild burst of applause and shouts of 'Bravo' from the audience.

Following the film the children were whisked away in the stretch limo. They travelled in convoy to the plush Fairmont Hotel. Crowds had gathered around the entrance to the hotel.

Luke was bewildered by what was going on. 'What's happening here?' he asked Todd.

'The Movie Ball. You'll really enjoy it. All the proceeds go to charity,' Todd replied casually. Todd walked over to some ecstatic girl fans standing behind the crash barrier to sign autographs. He obligingly signed their autograph books and chatted easily to them.

One of the girls held her book out and called to Luke, 'What about you?'

In astonishment Luke took the book and stared at it. 'What . . . what will I do?' he asked Todd.

Todd laughed and handed him a pen. 'Sign your name on it, silly.'

Luke's cheeks reddened as he scribbled his name on the autograph book and passed it back.

'Is that your first autograph?' teased Todd.

'Yeah,' said Luke feeling chuffed.

They continued on into the hotel. As they crossed the foyer a tall black man walked over to Todd. He shook the young star warmly by the hand. 'You have another success on your hands, young man.'

'Thank you, Mr Brown,' replied Todd. 'Can I introduce my friends from Ireland. Lads, this is Mayor Brown. Mayor, this is Luke, Sticky, Barbara, and Damian.'

The Mayor shook hands with each of them in turn and said, 'I hope you like our city.'

'I love it,' blurted Luke. 'It's the best place I've ever been in.'

The mayor threw his head back and laughed heartily. 'That's what I like to hear. Somebody sign this guy up to promote the city.'

The children mingled with the crowd, sipping coke as they chatted with well wishers.

Todd's parents led them down the palatial corridor to the conference room which was set out for dinner. Guests were taking their places at tables laid with an array of silverware and wine glasses.

'Now this is what I call stylish living,' remarked Mrs Carroll as she admired the splendour of the chandeliers. 'I'll never come down to earth again.'

'Yes, it has great character. The President often stays here. The view from the rooftop is breath-taking,' explained Mrs Harper as she consulted the menu.

Luke ran his eye over the menu. He plopped it down on the table with disgust. 'That's desperate. They've no burgers and chips,' he moaned.

His mother became cross. She spoke to him under her breath. 'Luke, don't make a show of us, for God's sake. Just pick something.'

Todd piped up next, 'I'd love burgers and chips too. Can we order them?'

Todd's mother checked him. 'Todd, what's going on?'

Todd gave Luke a tap on the leg under the table. 'Don't lose your cool, Mom. We're only kidding.'

There followed a sumptuous meal of a seafood platter, lobster bisque soup, fillet steak, baked Alaska and coffee.

Even Luke ate everything.

As they finished the meal Luke leaned back. He gave a loud belch. 'Oh excuse me,' he apologised, covering his mouth.

Following the meal a fifteen-piece orchestra took to the stage. They played a medley of tunes from Glen Miller to the Beatles to Oasis. Barbara and the boys danced together in a circle. Suddenly a man appeared behind Todd. He tapped him on the shoulder. 'Hi Todd, I was looking for you. I wanted to congratulate you on a great performance.'

'Oh thanks a lot, Tom. I'm glad you liked it,' said Todd, shaking the man's hand. Stickey stared and pointed at the man in a state of shock. He stammered, 'It's . . . it's . . . '

The other children glanced towards the man.

Luke's eyes opened wide. 'Tom . . . Tom Hanks,' he exclaimed.

'Are these your co-stars from Ireland?' smiled the star.

Todd pointed to each of the children as he named them. 'This is Luke, Sticky, Damian and Barbara.'

Tom Hanks shook hands with each of them in turn. 'Great to meet you all. I had a fantastic time in County Wexford a few years back making *Saving Private Ryan*.'

'That was a deadly film . . . all blood and guts,' said Luke, barely able to get the words out.

Tom Hanks wished them luck and moved away.

It was after two in the morning before Mrs Carroll and the Harpers could convince the children to leave. They talked non-stop on the way home and then sat around the kitchen for over an hour drinking cocoa and chatting excitedly, unable to end the night and go to bed.

12
FAREWELL

The rest of the holiday flew by and suddenly it was nearly time to go home. Today was their last day in San Francisco. Following their breakfast Gordon and Todd accompanied the Irish group into the city on a shopping expedition. Mrs Carroll had insisted that they all make out lists in advance. They bought calendars of the Golden Gate Bridge, sweatshirts and T-shirts with San Francisco logos, baseball caps, Ghirardelli chocolates, cookies and a musical cable car.

They finished their shopping spree with a visit to Macys self-service restaurant. The sign read: 'Eat as much as you like.' Luke didn't have to be told twice. He came back to their table with two plates laden with pizzas and pastas and a large coke.

'Oh, trust you, Luke,' said his mother with a sigh as she nibbled at a salad.

'Sure, you have to get value for your money,' replied Luke, through a mouthful of pizza. They finished the meal with an assortment of yoghurts, cookies and jelly.

That evening they all gathered in the dining room of the house for farewell drinks. There was an obvious air of sadness and nobody was very talkative. Todd left the room and returned minutes later with his arms laden.

'Hey, it's like Christmas,' cried Luke. 'Take a look at Todd. He looks like Santa.'

Todd presented each of the children with a collection of

large photographs which had been taken during their visit. There was also a video of *Orphans' Retreat,* along with stills and a poster of the film for each of them.

'Look, you can see us there,' said Damian, as he pointed to one of the stills.

'You look as scruffy as ever,' remarked Barbara.

'Thanks a million, Todd,' said Sticky. 'They must have cost you a bomb.'

'I have a little something else,' said Todd's father as he gave them all copies of the newspapers that covered their Alcatraz adventure.

'And don't forget these,' added his wife, handing them each a video. 'It's the video of you on the television news.'

'Oh deadly. We'll be able to show everybody at home,' yelled Luke.

Next morning it was with a degree of reluctance that Luke, Sticky and Damian packed their cases. Luke's case was so full that he had to sit on it to close the locks.

'Time doesn't half fly. It's desperate having to go back,' said Luke feeling in the dumps. Damian sighed. 'Yeah, school and all when we get back. It's the pits.'

Sticky was equally as gloomy. 'I'd give anything to live here all the time.'

Luke half smiled, 'Sun and heat all the time. Wouldn't it be massive.'

Damian slapped the top of his case and complained, 'Not like our poxy weather. Rain every day.'

'Sun and heat becomes boring at times,' smiled Todd's mother. 'Come on, downstairs everybody, it's time to go.'

Gordon packed the luggage into the boot of the stretch limo as the kids all said goodbye to Todd's parents.

Mrs Carroll bit her lip emotionally as she shook hands with Mrs Harper. 'No words can express how much I appreciate your kindness to the children and me. I'll always treasure memories of this trip.'

Mrs Harper clasped her hands. 'It's reward enough for us to see how happy Todd has been since his trip to Ireland. You don't realise how much pressure he is put under. You know he doesn't really have the life of a normal child. He speaks about Luke and the other children every day. .'

'That's lovely to hear. Our Luke is a bit of a scamp though. If you ever visit Ireland we would love to be able to return your hospitality,' said Mrs Carroll sincerely.

Mrs Harper nodded, 'We've heard so many favourable things about Ireland that we'll have to go over.'

'We can't wait,' added her husband. 'If it's half as good as we've heard it will be well worth the trip.'

Gordon clapped his hands. 'Chop, chop. All aboard. You don't want to miss your flight.'

The Irish visitors said goodbye for the final time and bundled into the vehicle with Todd and Gordon. The children waved out the rear window as the limo drove away from Sea Cliff. Conversation was minimal as they passed the familiar landmarks for the last time.

'Don't look so gloomy. You'll probably come back again,' said Todd in an attempt to cheer them up.

'I'll start saving right away,' said Luke hopefully. 'Every penny.'

The others nodded agreement.

They were soon at the airport. Gordon parked the limo and helped pack their luggage onto two trolleys. Then

Gordon and Todd accompanied them to the departure lounge. Tears welled up in Todd's eyes as he embraced and shook hands with each of them in turn.

'Thanks a million, Todd. It was the best holiday I've ever had. If I live to be a hundred I'll never forget it,' said Luke as he gave him a friendly punch on the arm.

Todd knew that he would burst into tears if he didn't leave them soon. 'If you don't get a move on they'll go without you.' He then gave Luke a high five. 'Keep it cool.'

On the return flight there was no jostling for positions. Mrs Carroll instructed that Sticky and Damian take the window seats. There were no objections. They all slept for most of the ten-hour flight. They only woke up to eat and drink.

It was lunchtime the following day when their flight touched down at Heathrow Airport. They transferred to Terminal One and took the homeward flight to Dublin.

They arrived mid-afternoon, bleary eyed and jet-lagged at a damp Dublin Airport. They yawned in turn as they pushed their trolleys into the arrivals lounge. Luke's father and Damian and Sticky's parents were there to greet them.

'Welcome back. You all have great tans,' said a pleased Mr Carroll.

'It's nice to be home,' sighed Mrs Carroll.

'You don't have to sound so cheerful,' muttered Luke.

Meanwhile, back in San Francisco, the old homeless man who had found the bag of money was enjoying his new-found wealth. Washed, clean-shaven and wearing a well-cut navy blue suit he was studying the gourmet lunch menu in the dining room of the St Francis Hotel.